A figure appeared at the top of the line of rock. It stood out blackly against the thinning yellow line of Jupiter. It was Summers, the man Council of Science Officer Lucky Starr had to bring back alive.

"Why have you turned against your own world, Summers?" Lucky called through his helmet radio. "What have the Sirians offered you? Money?"

"You won't catch me," he taunted. Summers' hands moved up to his helmet and he leaped backward and disappeared.

"He's dead," Lucky said grimly. "He had the answer we needed as to how much information the Sirians had, . . . poor fool."

"Poor traitor!" Bigman raged. "He wouldn't tell us, and now he can't!"

ISAAC ASIMOV

writing as Paul French

LUCKY STARR

and

THE MOONS OF JUPITER

A FAWCETT CREST BOOK

Fawcett Books, Greenwich, Connecticut

LUCKY STARR AND THE MOONS OF JUPITER

Published by Fawett Crest Books, CBS Publications, CBS
Consumer Publishing, a division of CBS, Inc., by arrange-
ment with Doubleday and Company, Inc.

ISBN: 0-449-23422-3

Printed in the United States of America

10   9   8   7   6   5   4   3   2   1

CONTENTS

Preface

Back in the 1950s, I wrote a series of six derring-do novels about David "Lucky" Starr and his battles against malefactors within the Solar System. Each of the six took place in a different region of the system and in each case I made use of the astronomical facts —as they were then known.

Now, a quarter-century later, Fawcett is bringing out the novels in new editions; but what a quarter-century it has been! More has been learned about the worlds of our Solar System in this last quarter-century than in all the thousands of years that went before.

LUCKY STARR AND THE MOONS OF JUPITER was written in 1956. In late 1973, however, the Jupiter-probe, Pioneer X, passed by Jupiter and recorded an enormous magnetic field containing dense concentrations of charged particles. The large satellites of Jupiter are buried in that field and the intensity of radiation would certainly make it difficult or even impossible for manned ships to maneuver in their neighborhood.

Lucky's trip through the satellite system would have to be adjusted to take the intense radiation into account if I were writing the book today. And in 1974, a 13th satellite of Jupiter was discovered, a very small one only a few miles across, with an orbit quite similar to that of Jupiter-IX. I'd have mentioned it if I were doing the book now.

I hope my Gentle Readers enjoy the book anyway, as an adventure story, but please don't forget that the advance of science can outdate even the most conscientious science-fiction writer and that my astronomical descriptions are no longer accurate in all respects.

ISAAC ASIMOV

1

Trouble on Jupiter Nine

Jupiter was almost a perfect circle of creamy light, half the apparent diameter of the moon as seen from Earth, but only one seventh as brightly lit because of its great distance from the sun. Even so, it was a beautiful and impressive sight.

Lucky Starr gazed at it thoughtfully. The lights in the control room were out and Jupiter was centered on the visiplate, its dim light making Lucky and his companion something more than mere shadows. Lucky said, "If Jupiter were hollow, Bigman, you could dump thirteen hundred planets the size of Earth into it and still not quite fill it up. It weighs more than all the other planets put together."

John Bigman Jones, who allowed no one to call him anything but Bigman, and who was five feet two inches tall if he stretched a little, disapproved of anything that was big, except Lucky. He said, "And what good is all of it? No one can land on it. No one can come near it."

"We'll never land on it, perhaps," said Lucky, "but we'll be coming close to it once the Agrav ships are developed."

"With the Sirians on the job," said Bigman, scowling in the gloom, "it's going to take *us* to make sure that happens."

"Well, Bigman, we'll see."

Bigman pounded his small right fist into the open palm of his other hand. "Sands of Mars, Lucky, how long do we have to wait here?"

They were in Lucky's ship, the *Shooting Starr,* which was in an orbit about Jupiter, having matched velocities with Jupiter Nine, the giant planet's outermost satellite of any size.

That satellite hung stationary a thousand miles away. Officially, its name was Adrastea, but except for the largest and closest, Jupiter's satellites were more popularly known by numbers. Jupiter Nine was only eighty-nine miles in diameter, merely an asteroid, really, but it looked larger than distant Jupiter, fifteen million miles away. The satellite was a craggy rock, gray and forbidding in the sun's weak light, and scarcely worth interest. Both Lucky and Bigman had seen a hundred such sights in the asteroid belt.

In one way, however, it was different. Under its skin a thousand men and billions of dollars labored to produce ships that would be immune to the effects of gravity.

Nevertheless, Lucky preferred watching Jupiter. Even at its present distance from the ship (actually three fifths of the distance of Venus from Earth at their closest approach), Jupiter showed a disc large enough to reveal its colored zones to the naked eye. They showed in faint pink and greenish-blue, as though a child had dipped his fingers in a watery paint and trailed them across Jupiter's image.

Lucky almost forgot the deadliness of Jupiter in its beauty. Bigman had to repeat his question in a louder voice.

"Hey, Lucky, how long do we have to wait here?"

"You know the answer to that, Bigman. Until Commander Donahue comes to pick us up."

"I know that part. What I want to know is why we have to wait for him."

"Because he's asked us to."

"Oh, he has. Who does the cobber think he is?"

"The head of the Agrav project," Lucky said patiently.

"You don't have to do what he says, you know, even if he is."

Bigman had a sharp and deep realization of Lucky's powers. As full member of the Council of Science, that selfless and brilliant organization that fought the enemies of Earth within and without the solar system, Lucky Starr could write his own ticket even against the most high-ranking.

But Lucky was not quite ready to do that. Jupiter was a known danger, a planet of poison and unbearable gravity; but the situation on Jupiter Nine was more dangerous still because the exact points of danger were unknown—and until Lucky could know a bit more, he was picking his way forward carefully.

"Be patient, Bigman," he said.

Bigman grumbled and flipped the lights on. "We're not staring at Jupiter all day, are we?"

He walked over to the small Venusian creature bobbing up and down in its enclosed water-filled cage in the corner of the pilot room. He peered fondly down at it, his wide mouth grinning with pleasure. The

V-frog always had that effect on Bigman, or indeed, on anyone.

The V-frog was a native of the Venusian oceans,* a tiny thing that seemed, at times, all eyes and feet. Its body was green and froglike and but six inches long. His two big eyes protruded like gleaming blackberries, and its sharp, strongly curved beak opened and closed at irregular intervals. At the moment its six legs were retracted, so that the V-frog hugged the bottom of its cage, but when Bigman tapped the top cover, they unfolded like a carpenter's rule and became stilts.

It was an ugly little thing but Bigman loved it when he was near it. He couldn't help it. Anyone else would feel the same. The V-frog saw to that.

Carefully Bigman checked the carbon-dioxide cylinder that kept the V-frog's water well saturated and healthful and made sure that the water temperature in the cage was at ninety-five. (The warm oceans of Venus were bathed by and saturated with an atmosphere of nitrogen and carbon dioxide. Free oxygen, nonexistent on Venus except in the man-made domed cities at the bottom of its ocean shallows, would have been most uncomfortable for the V-frog.)

Bigman said, "Do you think the weed supply is enough?" and as though the V-frog heard the remark, its beak snipped a green tendril off the native Venusian weed that spread through the cage, and chewed slowly.

Lucky said, "It will hold till we land on Jupiter Nine," and then both men looked up sharply as the receiving signal sounded its unmistakable rasp.

A stern, aging face was centered on the visiplate

* See *Lucky Starr and the Oceans of Venus.*

after Lucky's fingers had quickly made the necessary adjustments.

"Donahue at this end," said a voice briskly.

"Yes, Commander," said Lucky. "We've been waiting for you."

"Clear locks for tube attachment, then."

On the commander's face, written in an expression as clear as though it consisted of letters the size of Class I meteors, was worry—trouble and worry.

Lucky had grown accustomed to just that expression on men's faces in these past weeks. On Chief Councilman Hector Conway's for instance. To the chief councilman, Lucky was almost a son and the older man felt no need to assume any pretense of confidence.

Conway's rosy face, usually amiable and self-assured under its crown of pure white hair, was set in a troubled frown. "I've been waiting for a chance to talk to you for months."

"Trouble?" Lucky asked quietly. He had just returned from Mercury less than a month earlier, and the intervening time had been spent in his New York apartment. "I didn't get any calls from you."

"You earned your vacation," Conway said gruffly. "I wish I could afford to let it continue longer."

"Just what is it, Uncle Hector?"

The chief councilman's old eyes stared firmly into those of the tall, lithe youngster before him and seemed to find comfort in those calm, brown ones. "Sirius!" he said.

Lucky felt a stir of excitement within him. Was it the great enemy at last?

It had been centuries since the pioneering expeditions from Earth had colonized the planets of the nearer stars. New societies had grown up on those worlds outside the solar system. Independent societies that scarcely remembered their Earthly origin.

The Sirian planets formed the oldest and strongest of those societies. The society had grown up on new worlds where an advanced science was brought to bear on untapped resources. It was no secret that the Sirians, strong in the belief that they represented the best of mankind, looked forward to the time when they might rule all men everywhere; and that they considered Earth, the old mother world, their greatest enemy.

In the past they had done what they could to support the enemies of Earth at home* but never yet had they felt quite strong enough to risk open war.

But now?

"What's this about Sirius?" asked Lucky.

Conway leaned back. His fingers drummed lightly on the table. He said, "Sirius grows stronger each year. We know that. But their worlds are underpopulated; they have only a few millions. We still have more human beings in our solar system than exist in all the galaxy besides. We have more ships and more scientists; we still have the edge. But, by Space, we won't keep that edge if things keep on as they've been going."

"In what way?"

"The Sirians are finding out things. The Council has definite evidence that Sirius is completely up-to-date on our Agrav research."

"What!" Lucky was startled. There were few things more top-secret than the Agrav project. One of the reasons actual construction had been confined to one of the outer satellites of Jupiter had been for the sake

* See *Lucky Starr and the Pirates of the Asteroids.*

of better security. "Great Galaxy, how has that happened?"

Conway smiled bitterly. "That is indeed the question. How has that happened? All sorts of material are leaking out to them, and we don't know how. The Agrav data is most critical. We've tried to stop it. There isn't a man on the project that hasn't been thoroughly checked for loyalty. There isn't a precaution we haven't taken. Yet material still leaks. We've planted false data and that's gone out. We know it has from our own Intelligence information. We've planted data in such ways that it *couldn't* go out, and yet it has."

"How do you mean *couldn't* go out?"

"We scattered it so that no one man—in fact, no half dozen men—could possibly be aware of it all. Yet it went. It would mean that a number of men would have to be co-operating in espionage and that's just unbelievable."

"Or that some one man has access everywhere," said Lucky.

"Which is just as impossible. It must be something new, Lucky. Do you see the implication? If Sirius has learned a new way of picking our brains, we're no longer safe. We could never organize a defense against them. We could never make plans against them."

"Hold it, Uncle Hector. Great Galaxy, give yourself a minute. What do you mean when you say they're picking our brains?" Lucky fixed his glance keenly on the older man.

The chief councilman flushed. "Space, Lucky, I'm getting desperate. I can't see how else this can be done. The Sirians must have developed some form of mind reading, of telepathy."

"Why be embarrassed at suggesting that? I suppose

it's possible. We know of one practical means of telepathy at least. The Venusian V-frogs."

"All right," said Conway. "I've thought of that, too, but they don't have Venusian V-frogs. I know what's been going on in V-frog research. It takes thousands of them working in combination to make telepathy possible. To keep thousands of them anywhere but on Venus would be awfully difficult, and easily detectable, too. And without V-frogs, there is no way of managing telepathy."

"No way we've worked out," Lucky said softly, "so far. It is possible that the Sirians are ahead of us in telepathy research."

"Without V-frogs?"

"Even without V-frogs."

"I don't believe it," Conway cried violently. "I can't believe that the Sirians can have solved any problem that has left the Council of Science so completely helpless."

Lucky almost smiled at the older man's pride in the organization, but had to admit that there was something more than merely pride there. The Council of Science represented the greatest collection of intellect the galaxy had ever seen, and for a century not one sizable piece of scientific advance anywhere in the Galaxy had come anywhere but from the Council.

Nevertheless Lucky couldn't resist a small dig. He said, "They're ahead of us in robotics."

"Not really," snapped Conway. "Only in its applications. Earthmen invented the positronic brain that made the modern mechanical man possible. Don't forget that. Earth can take the credit for all the basic developments. It's just that Sirius builds more robots and," he hesitated, "has perfected some of the engineering details."

"So I found out on Mercury," Lucky said grimly.*

"Yes, I know, Lucky. That was dreadfully close."

"But it's over. Let's consider what's facing us now. The situation is this: Sirius is conducting successful espionage and we can't stop them."

"Yes."

"And the Agrav project is most seriously affected."

"Yes."

"And I suppose, Uncle Hector, that what you want me to do is to go out to Jupiter Nine and see if I can learn something about this."

Conway nodded gloomily. "It's what I'm asking you to do. It's unfair to you. I've gotten into the habit of thinking of you as my ace, my trump card, a man I can give any problem and be sure it will be solved. Yet what can you do here? There's nothing Council hasn't tried and we've located no spy and no method of espionage. What more can we expect of you?"

"Not of myself alone. I'll have help."

"Bigman?" The older man couldn't help smiling.

"Not Bigman alone. Let me ask you a question. To your knowledge, has any information concerning our V-frog research on Venus leaked out to the Sirians?"

"No," said Conway. "None has, to my knowledge."

"Then I'll ask to have a V-frog assigned to me."

"A V-frog! One V-frog?"

"That's right."

"But what good will that do you? The mental field of a single V-frog is terribly weak. You won't be able to read minds."

* See *Lucky Starr and the Big Sun of Mercury.*

"True, but I might be able to catch whiffs of strong emotion."

Conway said thoughtfully, "You might do that. But what good would that do?"

"I'm not sure yet. Still, it will be an advantage previous investigators haven't had. An unexpected emotional surge on the part of someone there might help me, might give me grounds for suspicion, might point the direction for further investigation. Then, too—"

"Yes?"

"If someone possesses telepathic power, developed either naturally or by use of artificial aids, I might detect something much stronger than just a whiff of emotion. I might detect an actual thought, some distinct thought, before the individual learns enough from my mind to shield his thoughts. You see what I mean?"

"He could detect your emotions, too."

"Theoretically, yes, but I would be listening for emotion, so to speak. He would not."

Conway's eyes brightened. "It's a feeble hope, but, by Space, it's a hope! I'll get you your V-frog . . . But one thing, David," and it was only at moments of deep concern that he used Lucky's real name, the one by which the young councilman had been known all through childhood—"I want you to appreciate the importance of this. If we don't find out what the Sirians are doing, it means they are really ahead of us at last. And *that* means war can't be delayed much longer. War or peace hangs on this."

"I know," said Lucky softly.

2

The Commander Is Angry

And so it came about that Lucky Starr, Earthman, and his small friend, Bigman Jones, born and bred on Mars,* traveled beyond the asteroid belt and into the outer reaches of the solar system. And it was for this reason also that a native of Venus, not a man at all, but a small mind-reading and mind-influencing animal, accompanied them.

They hovered, now, a thousand miles above Jupiter Nine and waited as a flexible conveyer tube was made fast between the *Shooting Starr* and the commander's ship. The tube linked air lock to air lock and formed a passageway which men could use in going from one ship to the other without having to put on a space suit. The air of both ships mingled, and a man used to space, taking advantage of the absence of gravity, could shoot along the tube after a single initial push and guide himself along those places where the tube curved with the gentle adjusting force of a well-placed elbow.

* See *David Starr, Space Ranger.*

The commander's hands were the first part of him visible at the lock opening. They gripped the lip of the opening and pushed in such a way that the commander himself leapfrogged out and came down in the *Shooting Starr*'s localized artificial gravity field (or pseudo-grav field, as it was usually termed) with scarcely a stagger. It was neatly done, and Bigman, who had high standards indeed for all forms of spacemen's techniques, nodded in approval.

"Good day, Councilman Starr," said Donahue gruffly. It was always a matter of difficulty whether to say "good morning," "good afternoon," or "good evening" in space, where, strictly speaking, there was neither morning, afternoon, nor evening. "Good day" was the neutral term usually adopted by spacemen.

"Good day, Commander," said Lucky. "Are there any difficulties concerning our landing on Jupiter Nine that account for this delay?"

"Difficulties? Well, that's as you look at it." He looked about and sat down on one of the small pilot's stools. "I've been in touch with Council headquarters but they say I must treat with you directly, so I'm here."

Commander Donahue was a wiry man, with an air of tension about him. His face was deeply lined, his hair grayish but showing signs of having once been brown. His hands had prominent blue veins along their backs, and he spoke in an explosive fashion, rapping out his phrases in a quick succession of words.

"Treat with me about what, sir?" asked Lucky.

"Just this, Councilman. I want you to return to Earth."

"Why, sir?"

The commander did not look directly at Lucky as he spoke. "We have a morale problem. Our men have been investigated and investigated *and* investigated. They've all come through clear each time, and each time a new investigation is started. They don't like it and neither would you. They don't like being under continual suspicion. And I'm completely on their side. Our Agrav ship is almost ready and this is not the time for my men to be disturbed. They talk of going on strike."

Lucky said calmly, "Your men may have been cleared but there is still leakage of information."

Donahue shrugged. "Then it must come from elsewhere. It must . . ." He broke off and a sudden incongruous note of friendliness entered his voice. "What's that?"

Bigman followed his eyes and said at once, "That's our V-frog, Commander, I'm Bigman."

The commander did not acknowledge the introduction. He approached the V-frog instead, staring into the enclosed water-filled cage. "That's a Venus creature, isn't it?"

"That's right," said Bigman.

"I've heard of them. Never saw one, though. Cute little jigger, isn't it?"

Lucky felt a grim amusement. He did not find it strange that in the midst of a most serious discussion the commander should veer off into an absorbed admiration for a small water creature from Venus. The V-frog itself made that inevitable.

The small creature was looking back at Donahue now out of its black eyes, swaying on its extensible legs and clicking its parrot beak gently. In all the known universe its means of survival was unique. It had no defensive weapons, no armor of any sort. It had no claws or teeth or horns. Its beak might bite, but even that bite could do no harm to any creature larger than itself.

Yet it multiplied freely along the weed-covered surface of the Venusian ocean, and none of the fierce predators of the ocean's deeps disturbed it, simply because the V-frog could control emotion. They instinctively caused all other forms of life to like them, to feel friendly toward them, to have no wish whatever to hurt them. So they survived. They did more than that. They flourished.

Now this particular V-frog was filling Donahue, quite obviously, with a feeling of friendliness, so that the army man pointed a finger at it through the glass of its cage and laughed to see it cock its head and sink down along its collapsing legs, as Donahue moved his finger downward.

"You don't suppose we could get a few of these for Jupiter Nine, do you, Starr?" he asked. "We're great ones for pets here. An animal here and there makes for a breath of home."

"It's not very practical," said Lucky. "V-frogs are difficult to keep. They have to be maintained in a carbon-dioxide-saturated system, you know. Oxygen is mildly poisonous to them. That makes things complicated."

"You mean they can't be kept in an open fish-bowl?"

"They can be at times. They're kept so on Venus, where carbon dioxide is dirt cheap and where they can always be turned loose in the ocean if they seem to be unhappy. On a ship, though, or on an airless world, you don't want to bleed carbon dioxide continuously into the air, so a closed system is best."

"Oh." The commander looked a bit wistful.

"To return to our original subject of discussion," said Lucky briskly, "I must refuse your suggestion that I leave. I have an assignment and I must carry it through."

It seemed to take a few seconds for the commander to emerge from the spell cast by the V-frog. His face darkened. "I'm sure you don't understand the entire situation." He turned suddenly, looking down at Bigman. "Consider your associate, for instance."

The small Martian, with a stiffening of spine, began to redden. "I'm Bigman," he said. "I told you that before."

"Not very big a man, nevertheless," said the commander.

And though Lucky placed a soothing hand on the little fellow's shoulder at once, it didn't help. Bigman cried, "Bigness isn't on the outside, mister. My name is Bigman, and I'm a big man against you or anyone you want to name regardless of what the yardstick says. And if you don't believe it . . ." He was shrugging his left shoulder vigorously. "Let go of me, Lucky, will you? This cobber here . . ."

"Will you wait just one minute, Bigman?" Lucky urged. "Let's find out what the commander is trying to say."

Donahue had looked startled at Bigman's sudden verbal assault. He said, "I'm sure I meant no harm in my remark. If I've hurt your feelings, I'm sorry."

"My feelings hurt?" said Bigman, his voice squeaking. "Me? Listen, one thing about me, I never lose my temper and as long as you apologize, we'll forget about it." He hitched at his belt and brought the palms of his hands down with a smart slap against the knee-high orange and vermilion boots that were the heritage of his Martian farm-boy past and without which he would never be seen in public (unless he substituted others with an equally garish color scheme).

"I want to be very plain with you, Councilman," said Donahue, turning to Lucky once more. "I have almost a thousand men here at Jupiter Nine, and they're tough, all of them. They have to be. They're far from home. They do a hard job. They run great risks. They have their own outlook on life now and it's a rough one. For instance, they haze newcomers and not with a light hand, either. Sometimes newcomers can't stand it and go home. Sometimes they're hurt. If they come through, everything's fine."

Lucky said, "Is this officially permitted?"

"No. But it is permitted unofficially. The men have to be kept happy somehow, and we can't afford to alienate them by interfering with their horseplay. Good men are hard to replace out here. Not many people are willing to come to the moons of Jupiter, you know. Then, too, the initiation is helpful in weeding out the misfits. Those that don't pass would probably fail in other respects eventually. That is why I made mention of your friend."

The commander raised his hands hurriedly. "Now make no mistake. I agree that he is big on the inside and capable and anything else you want. But will he be a match for what lies ahead? Will you, Councilman?"

"You mean the hazing?"

"It will be rough, Councilman," said Donahue. "The men know you are coming. News gets around somehow."

"Yes, I know," murmured Lucky.

The commander scowled. "In any case, they know you are to investigate them and they will feel no kindness toward you. They are in an ugly mood and they will hurt you, Councilman Starr. I am asking you not to land on Jupiter Nine for the project's sake, for my men's sake, and for your own. There you have it as plainly as I can put it."

Bigman stared at the change that came over Lucky. His usual look of calm good nature was gone. His dark brown eyes turned hard, and the straight lines of his lean and handsome face were set in something that Bigman rarely saw there: bitter anger. Every muscle of Lucky's tall body seemed tense.

Lucky said ringingly, "Commander Donahue, I am a member of the Council of Science. I am responsible only to the head of the Council and to the President of the Solar Federation of Worlds. I outrank you and you will be bound by my decisions and orders.

"I consider the warning you have just given me to be evidence of your own incompetence. Don't say anything, please; hear me out. You are obviously not in control of your men and not fit to command men. Now hear this: I will land on Jupiter Nine and I will conduct my investigations. I will handle your men if you cannot."

He paused while the other gasped and vainly attempted to find his voice. He rapped out, "Do you understand, Commander?"

Commander Donahue, his face congested almost beyond recognition, managed to grind out, "I will take this up with the Council of Science. No arrogant young whipsnap can talk like that to me, councilman or no councilman. I will match my record as a leader of men against that of anyone in the service. Furthermore, my warning to you will be on record also and if you are hurt on Jupiter Nine, I will run the risk of court-martial gladly. I will do nothing for you. In fact, I hope—I hope they teach you manners, you . . ."

He was past speech once more. He turned on his heel, toward the open lock, connected still with the space tube to his own ship. He clambered in, missing a hand hold in his anger and stumbling badly.

Bigman watched with awe as the commander's heels disappeared down the tube. The other's anger had been so intense a thing that the little Martian had seemed to feel it in his own mind as though waves of heat were rolling in upon him.

Bigman said, "Wow, that cobber was really *going!* You had him rocking."

Lucky nodded. "He was angry. No doubt about it."

Bigman said, "Listen, maybe *he's* the spy. He'd know the most. He'd have the best chance."

"He'd also be the most thoroughly investigated, so your theory is doubtful. But at least he's helped us out in a little experiment, so when I see him next I will have to apologize."

"Apologize?" Bigman was horrified. It was his firm view that apologies were strictly something that other people had to do. "Why?"

"Come, Bigman, do you suppose I really meant those things I said?"

"You weren't angry?"

"Not really."

"It was an act?"

"You could call it that. I wanted to make him angry, really angry, and I succeeded. I could tell that first-hand."

"Firsthand?"

"Couldn't you? Couldn't you feel the anger just pouring out of him all over you?"

"Sands of Mars! The V-frog!"

"Of course. It received the commander's anger and rebroadcast it on to us. I had to know if one V-frog could do it. We tested it back on Earth, but until I tried it under actual field conditions, I wasn't sure. Now I am."

"It broadcast fine."

"I know. So at least it proves we have a weapon, one weapon, after all."

3

The Agrav Corridor

"Good deal," said Bigman fiercely. "Then we're on our way."

"Hold it," said Lucky at once. "Hold everything, my friend. This is a non-specific weapon. We'll sense strong emotion but we may never sense one that will give us the key to the mystery. It's like having eyes. We may see, but we may not see the right thing, not ever."

"*You* will," said Bigman confidently.

Dropping down toward Jupiter Nine reminded Bigman very strongly of similar maneuvers in the asteroid belt. As Lucky had explained on the voyage outward, most astronomers considered Jupiter Nine to have been a true asteroid to begin with; a rather large one that had been captured by Jupiter's tremendous gravity field many millions of years previously.

In fact, Jupiter had captured so many asteroids that here, fifteen million miles from the giant planet, there was a kind of miniature asteroid belt belonging to Jupiter alone. The four largest of these asteroid satellites, each from forty to a hundred miles in diameter, were

Jupiter Twelve, Eleven, Eight, and Nine. In addition there were at least a hundred additional satellites of more than a mile in diameter, unnumbered and unregarded. Their orbits had been plotted only in the last ten years when Jupiter Nine was first put to use as an anti-gravity research center, and the necessity of traveling to and from it had made the population of surrounding space important.

The approaching satellite swallowed the sky and became a rough world of peaks and rocky channels, unsoftened by any touch of air in the billions of years of its history. Bigman, still thoughtful, said, "Lucky, why in Space do they call this Jupiter Nine, anyway? It isn't the ninth one out from Jupiter according to the Atlas. Jupiter Twelve is a lot closer."

Lucky smiled. "The trouble with you, Bigman, is that you're spoiled. Just because you were born on Mars, you think mankind has been cutting through space ever since creation. Look boy, it's only a matter of a thousand years since mankind invented the first spaceship."

"I know that," said Bigman indignantly. "I'm not ignorant. I've had schooling. Don't go shoving your big brain all over the place."

Lucky's smile expanded, and he rapped Bigman's skull with two knuckles. "Anybody home?"

Bigman's fist whipped toward Lucky's abdomen, but Lucky caught it in midair and held the little fellow motionless.

"It's as simple as this, Bigman. Before space travel was invented, men were restricted to Earth and all they knew about Jupiter was what they could see in a telescope. The satellites are numbered in the order they were discovered, see?"

"Oh," said Bigman, and yanked free. "Poor ancestors!" He laughed, as he always did, at the thought of human beings cooped up on one world, peering out longingly, even as he struggled to free himself from Lucky's grip.

Lucky went on. "The four big satellites of Jupiter are numbered One, Two, Three, and Four, of course, but the numbers are hardly ever used. The names Io, Europa, Ganymede, and Callisto are familiar names. The nearest satellite of all, a small one, is Jupiter Five, while the farther ones have numbers up to Twelve. The ones past Twelve weren't discovered till after space travel was invented and men had reached Mars and the asteroid belt . . . Watch out now. We've got to adjust for landing."

It was amazing, thought Lucky, how you could consider tiny a world eighty-nine miles in diameter as long as you were nowhere near it. Of course, such a world is tiny compared to Jupiter or even to Earth. Place it gently on Earth and its diameter is small enough to allow it to fit within the state of Connecticut without lapping over; and its surface area is less than that of Pennsylvania.

And yet, just the same, when you came to enter the small world, when you found your ship enclosed in a large lock and moved by gigantic grapples (working against a gravitational force of almost zero but against full inertia) into a large cavern capable of holding a hundred ships the size of the *Shooting Starr*, it no longer seemed so small.

And then when you came across a map of Jupiter Nine on the wall of an office and studied the network of underground caverns and corridors within which a complicated program was being carried out, it began to seem actually large. Both horizontal and vertical projections of the work volume of Jupiter Nine were shown on the map, and though only a small portion of the satellite was being used, Lucky could see that some of the corridors penetrated as much as two miles beneath the surface and that others spread out just under the surface for nearly a hundred miles.

"A tremendous job," he said softly to the lieutenant at his side.

Lieutenant Augustus Nevsky nodded briefly. His uniform was spotless and gleaming. He had a stiff little blond mustache, and his wide-set blue eyes had a habit of staring straight ahead as though he were at perpetual attention.

He said with pride, "We're still growing."

He had introduced himself a quarter of an hour earlier, as Lucky and Bigman had stepped from the ship, as the personal guide assigned them by Commander Donahue.

Lucky said with some amusement, "Guide? Or guardian, Lieutenant? You are armed."

Any trace of feeling was carefully washed out of the other's face. "My arms are regulation for officers on duty, Councilman. You will find you will need a guide here."

But he seemed to relax, and there was ordinary human feeling about him as he listened to the visitors' awed praise of the project. He said, "Of course the absence of any significant gravitational field makes certain engineering tricks feasible that wouldn't work on

Earth. Underground corridors require practically no support."

Lucky nodded, then said, "I understand that the first Agrav ship is about ready for take-off."

The lieutenant said nothing for a moment. His face blanked free, again, of emotion or feeling. Then he said stiffly, "I will show you your quarters first. It can be most easily reached by Agrav, if I can persuade you to use an Agrav cor—"

"Hey, Lucky," called Bigman in sudden excitement. "Look at this."

Lucky turned. It was only a half-grown cat, gray as smoke, with the look of solemn sadness that cats usually have, and a back that arched readily against Bigman's curved fingers. She was purring.

Lucky said, "The commander said they went for pets here. Is this one yours, Lieutenant?"

The officer flushed. "We all have shares in it. There are a few other cats around, too. They come on the supply ships sometimes. We've got some canaries, a parakeet, white mice, goldfish. Things like that. Nothing like your whatever-it-is, though." And his eyes, as they looked quickly at the V-frog's bowl tucked under Lucky's arm, contained a spark of envy.

But Bigman was concentrating on the cat. There was no native animal life on Mars and the furry pets of Earth always had the charm of novelty to him.

"He likes me, Lucky."

"It's a she," said the lieutenant, but Bigman paid no attention. The cat, tail hoisted into a stiff vertical with only the tip drooping, walked past him, doubling sharply so as to present first one side, then the other, to Bigman's gentle stroking.

And then the purring stopped, and through Bigman's mind stabbed one pure touch of fevered and hungry desire.

It startled him for a moment, and then he noticed that the cat had stopped purring and was squatting slightly in the tense hunting posture dictated by its millions-of-years-old instincts.

Her green slitted eyes stared directly at the V-frog.

But the emotion, so feline in its touch, was gone almost as soon as it had come. The cat padded softly over to the glass container Lucky was holding and stared in curiously, purring with contentment.

The cat, too, liked the V-frog. It had to.

Lucky said, "You were saying, Lieutenant, we would have to reach our quarters by Agrav. Were you going to explain what that means?"

The lieutenant, who had also been staring fondly at the V-frog, paused to gather his wits before answering. "Yes. It's simple enough. We have artificial gravity fields here on Jupiter Nine as on any asteroid or on any space ship for that matter. They are arranged at each of the main corridors, end to end, so that you can fall the length of them in either direction. It's like dropping straight down a hole on Earth."

Lucky nodded. "How fast do you drop?"

"Well, that's the point. Ordinarily, gravity pulls constantly and you fall faster and faster . . ."

"Which is why I ask my question," interposed Lucky dryly.

"But not under Agrav controls. Agrav is really A-grav: no gravity, you see. Agrav can be used to absorb gravitational energy or store it or transfer it. The point is you only fall so fast, you see, and no faster.

With a gravitational field in the other direction, too, you can even slow down. An Agrav corridor with two pseudo-grav fields is very simple and it has been used as a steppingstone to an Agrav ship which works in a single gravitational field. Now Engineers' Quarters, which is where your rooms will be, is only a little over a mile from here and the most direct route is by Corridor A-2. Ready?"

"We will be once you explain how we're to work Agrav."

"That's hardly a problem." Lieutenant Nevsky presented each with a light harness, adjusting them over the shoulders and at the waist, talking rapidly about the controls.

And then he said, "If you'll follow me, gentlemen, the corridor is just a few yards in this direction."

Bigman hesitated at the opening of the corridor. He was not afraid of space in itself, or of drops in themselves. But all his life he had been used to bridging gaps under Martian gravity or less. This time the pseudo-grav field was at full Earth-normal, and under its influence the corridor was a brilliantly lighted hole, plummeting, apparently, straight downward, even though in actuality (Bigman's mind told him) it paralleled the satellite's surface closely.

The lieutenant said, "Now this is the lane for travel in the direction of Engineers' Quarters. If we were to approach from the other side, 'down' would appear to be in the other direction. Or we could make 'up' and 'down' change places by appropriate adjustments of our Agrav controls."

He looked at the expression on Bigman's face and

said, "You'll get the idea as you go along. It becomes second nature after a while."

He stepped into the corridor and didn't drop an inch. It was as though he were standing on an invisible platform.

He said earnestly, "Have you set the dial at zero?"

Bigman did so, and instantly all sensation of gravity vanished. He stepped into the corridor.

Now the lieutenant's hand on the central knob of his own controls turned it sharply, and he sank, gathering speed. Lucky followed him, and Bigman, who would sooner have fallen the length of the corridor under double gravity and been smashed to pulp than fail to do anything Lucky did, took a deep breath and let himself fall.

"Turn back to zero," called the lieutenant, "and you'll be moving at constant velocity. Get the feel of it."

Periodically they approached and passed through luminous green letters that glowed KEEP TO THIS SIDE. Once there was the flash of a man passing (falling, really) in the other direction. He was moving much more rapidly than they were.

"Are there ever any collisions, Lieutenant?" asked Lucky.

"Not really," said the lieutenant. "The experienced dropper watches for people who might be overtaking him or whom he might be overtaking, and it's easy enough to slow down or speed up. Of course the boys will bump on purpose sometimes. It's a kind of rowdy fun that ends with a broken collarbone sometimes." He looked quickly at Lucky. "Our boys play rough."

Lucky said, "I understand. The commander warned me."

Bigman, who had been staring downward through the well-lit tunnel into which he was sinking, cried in sudden exhilaration, "Hey, Lucky, this is fun when you get used to it," and turned his controls into the positive region.

He sank faster, his head moving down to a level with Lucky's feet, then farther down at an increasing rate.

Lieutenant Nevsky cried out in instant alarm, "Stop that, you fool. Turn back into the negatives!"

Lucky called out an imperious, "Bigman, slow down!"

They caught up to him, the lieutenant angrily exclaiming. "Don't ever do that! There are all sort of barriers and partitions along these corridors, and if you don't know your way, you'll be slamming into one just when you think you're safe."

"Here, Bigman," said Lucky. "Hold the V-frog. That will give you some responsibility and make you behave, perhaps."

"Aw, Lucky," said Bigman, abashed. "I was just kicking my heels a bit. Sands of Mars, Lucky . . ."

"All right," said Lucky. "No harm done," and Bigman brightened at once.

Bigman looked down again. Falling at a constant rate was not quite the same as free fall in space. In space, nothing seemed to move. A space ship might be traveling at a velocity of hundreds of thousands of miles an hour and there would still be the sensation of motionlessness all about. The distant stars never moved.

Here, though, the sense of motion was all about. The lights and openings and various attachments that lined the corridor walls flashed past.

In space, one expected that there would be no "up"

and "down," but here there was none either and it
seemed wrong. As long as he looked "down" past his
feet, it seemed "down" and that was all right. When he
looked "up," however, there would be a quick sensation that "up" was really "down," that he was standing
head downward falling "up." He looked toward his feet
again quickly to get rid of the sensation.

The lieutenant said, "Don't bend too far forward,
Bigman. The Agrav works to keep you lined up in the
direction of fall, but if you bend over too much, you'll
start tumbling."

Bigman straightened.

The lieutenant said, "There's nothing fatal about
tumbling. Anyone who's used to Agrav can straighten
himself out again. Beginners would find it troublesome,
however. We'll decelerate now. Move the dial into the
negatives and keep it there. About minus five."

He was slowing as he spoke, moving above them.
His feet dangled at Bigman's eye level.

Bigman moved the dial, trying desperately to line
himself up with the lieutenant. And as he slowed, "up"
and "down" became definite, and in the wrong way.
He *was* standing on his head.

He said, "Hey, the blood's rushing to my head."

The lieutenant said sharply, "There are footholds
along the sides of the corridor. Hook one with the toe
of your foot as you reach it and let go quickly."

He did so as he said this. His head swung outward,
and head and feet reversed position. He continued
swinging and stopped himself with a quick hand tap
against the wall.

Lucky followed suit, and Bigman, flailing widely with
his short legs, managed to catch one of the footholds

at last. He whirled sharply and caught the wall with his elbow just a trifle too hard for comfort but managed to line up properly.

At least he was head-up again. He wasn't falling any more, but rising, as though he had been shot out of a cannon and rising against gravity more and more slowly; but at least he was head-up.

When they were moving at a slow crawl, Bigman, looking uneasily toward his feet, thought: We're going to be falling again. And suddenly the corridor looked like an endlessly deep well and his stomach tightened.

But the lieutenant said, "Adjust to zero," and at once they stopped slowing down. They just moved upward, as though in a smooth, slow elevator, until they reached a cross-level at which the lieutenant, seizing a foothold with one toe, brought himself to a feathery stop.

"Engineers' Quarters, gentlemen," he said.

"And," added Lucky Starr gently, "a reception committee."

For men were waiting for them in the corridor now, fifty of them at least.

Lucky said, "You said they liked to play rough, Lieutenant, and maybe they want to play now."

He stepped firmly out into the corridor. Bigman, nostrils flaring with excitement and grateful to be on the firm pseudo-grav of a solid floor, clutched the V-frog's cage tightly and was at Lucky's heels, facing the waiting men of Jupiter Nine.

4

Initiation!

Lieutenant Nevsky tried to make his voice crackle with authority as he placed his hand on the butt of his blaster. "What are you men doing here?"

There was a small murmur from the men, but by and large they remained quiet. Eyes turned to the one of them who stood in front, as though they were waiting for him to speak.

The leader of the men was smiling, and his face was crinkled into an expression of apparent good will. His straight hair, parted in the middle, had a light-orange tint to it. His cheekbones were broad and he chewed gum. His clothing was of synthetic fiber, as was true of that of the others, but unlike the others', his shirt and trousers were ornamented with brass buttons that were large and bulky. Four on his shirt front, one each on the two shirt pockets, and four down the side of each pants leg: fourteen altogether. They seemed to serve no purpose; to be only for show.

"All right, Summers," said the lieutenant, turning to this man, "what are the men doing here?"

Summers spoke now in a soft, wheedling voice.

"Well, now, Lieutenant, we thought it would be nice to meet the new man. He'll be seeing a lot of us. He'll be asking questions. Why shouldn't we meet him now?"

He looked at Lucky Starr as he spoke, and for a moment there was a touch of ice in that glance that swallowed up all the show of softness.

The lieutenant said, "You men should be at work."

"Have a heart, Lieutenant," said Summers, chewing even more slowly and leisurely. "We've *been* working. Now we want to say hello."

The lieutenant was obviously uncertain as to his next move. He looked doubtfully at Lucky.

Lucky said, "Which rooms are to be ours, Lieutenant?"

"Rooms 2A and 2B, sir. To find them—"

"I'll find them. I'm sure one of these men will direct me. And now, Lieutenant Nevsky, that you've directed us to our quarters, I think your assignment is completed. I'll be seeing you again."

"I can't leave!" said Lieutenant Nevsky in a low, appalled whisper.

"I think you can."

"Sure you can, Lieutenant," said Summers, grinning more broadly than ever. "A simple hello won't hurt the boy." There was a snicker of laughter from the men behind him. "And besides, you've been asked to leave."

Bigman approached Lucky and muttered in an urgent whisper. "Lucky, let me give the V-frog to the lieutenant. I can't fight and hold it, too."

"You just hold it," said Lucky. "I want it exactly here. . . . Good day, Lieutenant. Dismissed!"

The lieutenant hesitated, and Lucky said in a tone

that, for all its softness, bit like steel. "That's an order, Lieutenant."

Lieutenant Nevsky's face assumed a soldierly rigidity. He said sharply, "Yes, sir."

Then, surprisingly, he hesitated one further moment and glanced down at the V-frog in the crook of Bigman's arm, as it chewed idly at a fern frond. "Take care of that little thing." He turned and was in the Agrav corridor in two steps, disappearing almost at once in a rush of speed.

Lucky turned to face the men again. He was under no illusions. They were grim-faced and they meant business, but unless he could face them down and prove that he meant business as well, his mission would come to nothing against the rock of their hostility. He would have to win them over somehow.

Summers' smile had become the least bit wolfish. He said, "Well, now, friend, the uniform-boy is gone. We can talk. I'm Red Summers. What's your name?"

Lucky smiled in return. "My name is David Starr. My friend's name is Bigman."

"Seems to me I heard you called Lucky when all that whispering was going on a while back."

"I'm called Lucky by my friends."

"Isn't that nice. Do you want to stay lucky?"

"Do you know a good way?"

"Matter of fact, Lucky Starr, I do." Suddenly his face contorted itself into a bitter scowl. "Get off Jupiter Nine."

There was a hoarse roar of approval from the others, and a few voices took up the cry of "Get off! Get off!"

They crowded closer, but Lucky stood his ground. "I have important reasons to stay on Jupiter Nine."

"In that case, I'm afraid you aren't lucky," said Summers. "You're a greenhorn and you look soft, and soft greenhorns get hurt on Jupiter Nine. We worry about you."

"I think I won't get hurt."

"That's what you think, eh?" said Summers. "Armand, come here."

From the ranks behind him, a huge man stepped forward, round-faced, beefy of build, with large shoulders and a barrel chest. He topped Lucky's six feet one by half a head and looked down at the young councilman with a smile that showed yellowed, wide-spaced teeth.

The men were beginning to take seats on the floor. They shouted to one another with lighthearted cheer, as though they were about to watch a ball game.

One called out, "Hey, Armand, watch out you don't step on the kid!"

Bigman started, and glared furiously in the direction of the voice but could not identify the speaker.

Summers said, "You could still leave, Starr."

Lucky said, "I have no intention of doing so, particularly at a moment when you seem to be planning some sort of entertainment."

"Not for you," said Summers. "Now listen, Starr, we're ready for you. We've been ready since we got word that you were coming. We've had enough of you little tinhorns from Earth and we aren't taking any more. I've got men stationed on various levels. We'll know if the commander tries to interfere, and if he does, then by Jupiter, we're ready to go on strike. Am I right, men?"

"Right!" came back the multiple roar.

"And the commander knows it," said Summers, "and I don't think he'll interfere. So this gives us our chance to give you our initiation and after that I'll ask you again if you want to leave. If you're conscious, that is."

"You're going to a lot of trouble for nothing," said Lucky. "What harm am I doing you?"

"You won't be doing us any," said Summers. "I guarantee that."

Bigman said, in his tense, high-pitched voice, "Look, you cobber, you're talking to a councilman. Have you stopped to figure what happens if you fool with the Council of Science?"

Summers looked at him suddenly, put his fists on his hips, and bent his head back to laugh. "Hey, men, it talks. I was wondering what it was. It looks as though Lucky Snoop has brought along his baby brother for protection."

Bigman went dead-white, but under the cover of the laughter Lucky stooped and spoke through stiff lips. "Your job is to hang on to the V-frog, Bigman. I'll take care of Summers. And, Great Galaxy, Bigman, stop broadcasting anger! I can't get a thing on the V-frog except that."

Bigman swallowed hard twice, three times.

Summers said softly, "Now, Councilman Snoop, can you maneuver under Agrav?"

"I just have, Mr. Summers."

"Well, we'll just have to test you and make sure. We can't have anyone around who hasn't learned all the Agrav ropes. It's too dangerous. Right, men?"

"Right!" they roared again.

"Armand here," said Summers, and his hand rested

on one of Armand's huge shoulders, "is our best teacher. You'll know all about Agrav maneuvering when you're through with him. Or you will know if you stay out of his way. I suggest you get out into the Agrav corridor now. Armand will join you."

Lucky said, "If I choose not to go?"

"Then we'll throw you into the corridor anyway and Armand goes after you."

Lucky nodded. "You seem determined. Are there any rules to this lesson I'm going to get?"

There was wild laughter, but Summers held up his arms. "Just keep out of Armand's way, Councilman. That's the only rule you'll have to remember. We'll be at the lip of the corridor watching. If you try to crawl out of Agrav before you've completed your lesson, we'll throw you back in, and there are men stationed at other levels, watching, and they're ready to do the same."

Bigman cried, "Sands of Mars, your man outweighs Lucky by fifty pounds and he's an expert with Agrav!"

Summers turned on him in mock surprise. *"No!* I never thought of that. What a shame!" There was laughter from the men. "On your way, Starr. Get into the corridor, Armand. Drag him in if you have to."

"He won't have to," said Lucky. He turned and moved into the open space of the wide Agrav corridor. As his feet drifted out into empty air, his fingers caught gently at the wall, twisting him in a slow, turning motion that he stopped with another touch against the wall. He stood there in midair, facing the men.

There was some murmuring at Lucky's maneuver, and Armand nodded, speaking for the first time in a rolling appreciative bass. "Hey, mister, that's not bad."

Summers, lips suddenly set and with a frown newly

creasing his forehead, struck Armand a sharp blow on the back. "Don't talk, you idiot! Get in after him and give it to him."

Armand moved forward slowly. He said, "Hey, Red, let's not make too much of this."

Summers' face contorted in fury. "Get in there! And you do what I said. I told you what he is. If we don't get rid of him, they'll be sending more." His words were a harsh whisper that didn't carry.

Armand stepped into the corridor and stood face to face with Lucky.

Lucky Starr waited in what was almost absence of mind. He was concentrating on the faint whiffs of emotion brought him by the V-frog. Some he could recognize without difficulty, both as to their nature and their owner. Red Summers was easiest to detect: fear and niggling hate mixed with an undertone of anxious triumph. Armand loosed a small leak of tension. Occasionally there were sharp pinpoints of excitement from one or another, and sometimes Lucky could identify the owner because it coincided with a happy shout or a threatening one. All of it had to be sorted out from the steady trickle of Bigman's anger, of course.

But now he was staring into Armand's small eyes and he was aware that the other was bobbing up and down, a few inches either way. Armand's hand fingered his chest control.

Lucky was instantly alert. The other was alternating the gravitational direction, moving the controls this way and that. Was he expecting to confuse Lucky?

Lucky was sharply aware that for all his experience with space he was inexperienced in the type of weight-

lessness brought about by Agrav, for this was a weight-
lessness that wasn't absolute, as in space, but one that
could be changed at will.

And suddenly Armand dropped as though he had
stepped through a trap door—except that he dropped
upward!

As Armand's large legs moved up past Lucky's head,
they parted and came together as if to catch Lucky's
head in a vise.

Automatically Lucky's head snapped back, but as it
did so, his legs moved forward, his body swinging about
its center of gravity, and for a moment, he was off bal-
ance and flailing helplessly. A roar of laughter arose
from the watching men.

Lucky knew what was wrong. He should have
dodged by gravity. If Armand moved up, Lucky should
have adjusted controls to move up with him or to race
down past him. And now it would take the pull of gravity to straighten him out. At gravity zero, he would
tumble indefinitely.

But before his fingers could touch his controls, Armand was past the top of his rise and was gathering
speed downward. As he dropped past Lucky once
more, his elbow caught Lucky a sharp jab in the hip.
He dropped farther and his thick fingers clutched at
Lucky's ankles, carrying him down, down. Armand
pulled strongly downward and reached up to seize
Lucky's shoulders. His harsh breath stirred Lucky's
hair. He said, "You need a lot of training, mister."

Lucky brought up his own arms head-high and broke
the other's hold sharply.

Lucky dialed gravity up and helped his upward
movement by bringing his foot sharply down on the

other's shoulder, accelerating his own pace and slowing the other's. To his own senses it now seemed that he was falling head downward and there was a tenseness about that sensation that seemed to be slowing his reactions. Or was it his Agrav controls which were somewhat sluggish? He tested them and lacked the experience to be certain, yet felt that they were.

Armand was on him now, bellowing, thrusting against him, attempting to use his own greater mass of body to maneuver Lucky hard against the wall.

Lucky wriggled his hand toward the controls in order to reverse the direction of gravity. He readied his knees for an upward thrust to coincide and lurch Armand out of position.

But it was Armand's field that shifted first, and it was Lucky who was lurched out of position.

Armand's feet shot backward now, striking the wall of the corridor as it was flashing by and angling the pair, by recoil, against the opposite wall. Lucky struck bruisingly and skidded along it some feet before his ankle caught one of the metal railings and his body swung away and into the open corridor.

Armand whispered hotly in Lucky's ear, "Had enough, mister? Just tell Red you'll leave. I don't want to hurt you bad."

Lucky shook his head. Strange, he thought, that Armand's gravitational field had beaten his own to the shift. He had felt Armand's hand move to the controls and he was certain his own controls had moved first.

Twisting suddenly, Lucky placed his elbow sharply in the pit of Armand's stomach. Armand grunted, and in that split second Lucky got his legs between himself and the other's and straightened them. The two men flew apart and Lucky was free.

He shot away an instant before Armand returned, and then for the next few minutes Lucky concentrated only on staying away. He was learning the use of the controls and they *were* sluggish. It was only by skillful use of the footholds along the walls and lightning-like head-to-foot reversals that he managed to avoid Armand.

And then while he was drifting feather-fashion, allowing Armand to shoot past him, he turned his Agrav controls and found no response at all. There was no change in the gravitational field direction; no sudden sensation of accelerating one way or the other.

Instead, Armand was on him again, grunting, and Lucky found himself crashing with stunning force against the corridor wall.

5

Needle-Guns and Neighbors

Bigman felt fully confident of Lucky's ability to handle any overgrown mass of beef, and though he felt a sharp anger at the unsympathetic crowd, he felt no fear.

Summers had approached the lip of the corridor and so had another, a gangling, dark-complexioned fellow who barked out events as they occurred in a raucous voice, as though it were a flight-polo game on the subetherics.

There were cheers when Armand first slammed Lucky against the corridor wall. Bigman discounted those with contempt. Of course that shouting fool would try to make it look good for his own side. Wait till Lucky got the feel of the Agrav technique; he would cut that Armand guy into ribbons. Bigman was sure of it.

But then when the dark fellow yelled, "Armand has him now in a head lock. He's maneuvering for a second fall; feet against the wall; retract and extend and *there's the crash, a beauty!*" Bigman felt the beginnings of uneasiness.

He edged close to the corridor himself. No one paid

any attention to him. It was one advantage of his small size. People who didn't know him tended to discount him as a possible danger, to ignore him.

Bigman looked down and saw Lucky pushing away from the wall, Armand drifting nearby, waiting.

"Lucky!" he yelled shrilly. "Stay away!"

His cry was lost in the hubbub, but the dark man's voice as it was lowered in a conversational aside to Red Summers was not. Bigman caught it.

The dark man said, "Give the snoop some power, Red. There won't be any excitement."

And Summers growled in response, "I don't want excitement. I want Armand to finish the job."

Bigman didn't get the significance of the short exchange for a moment, but only for a moment. And then his eyes darted sharply in the direction of Red Summers, whose hands, held closely against his chest, were manipulating some small object Bigman could not identify.

"Sands of Mars!" Bigman cried breathlessly. He sprang back. "You! Summers! You foul-fighting cobber!"

This was another one of those times when Bigman was glad he carried a needle-gun even in the face of Lucky's disapproval. Lucky considered it an unreliable weapon, as it was too hard to focus accurately, but Bigman would sooner doubt the fact that he was as tall as any six-footer as doubt his own skill.

When Summers didn't turn at Bigman's shout, Bigman clenched his fist about the weapon (of which only half-inch of snout, narrowing to a needlepoint, showed between the second and third fingers of his right hand) and squeezed just tightly enough to activate it.

Simultaneously there was a flash of light six inches in front of Summers' nose, and a slight pop. It was not very impressive. Only air molecules were being ionized. Summers jumped, however, and panic, transmitted by the V-frog, rose sharply.

"Everybody," called Bigman. "Freeze! *Freeze!* You split-head, underlipped miseries." Another needle-gun discharge popped the air, this time over Summers' head where all could see it plainly.

Few people might have handled needle-guns, which were expensive and hard to get licenses for, but everybody knew what a needle-gun discharge looked like, if only from subetheric programs, and everyone knew the damage it could do.

It was as though fifty men had stopped breathing.

Bigman was bathed in the cold drizzle of human fear from fifty frightened men. He backed against the wall.

He said, "Now listen, all of you. How many of you know that this cobber Summers is gimmicking my friend's Agrav controls? This fight is fixed!"

Summers said desperately, through clenched teeth, "You're wrong. You're wrong."

"Am I? You're a brave man, Summers, when you've got fifty against two. Let's see you stay brave against a needle-gun. They're hard to aim, of course, and I might miss."

He clenched his fist again, and this time the pop of the discharge was sharply ear-splitting and the flash dazzled all the spectators but Bigman, who, of them all, was the only one who knew exactly when to close his eyes for a moment.

Summers emitted a strangled yell. He was untouched except that the top button on his shirt was gone.

Bigman said, "Nice aiming if I do say so myself, but I suppose having a run of luck is too much to ask. I'd advise you not to move, Summers. Pretend you're stone, you cobber, because if you do move, I'll miss and feeling a chunk of your skin go will hurt you worse than just losing a button."

Summers closed his eyes. His forehead was glistening with perspiration. Bigman calculated the distance and clenched twice.

Pow! Smack! Two more buttons gone.

"Sands of Mars, my lucky day! Isn't it nice that you've arranged to have no one come around to interfere? Well, one more—for the road."

And this time Summers yelled in agony. There was a rent in the shirt and reddened skin showed.

"Aw," said Bigman, "not on the nose. Now I'm rattled and I'll probably miss the next by two inches . . . Unless you're ready to say something, Summers."

"All right," yelled the other. "I've fixed it."

Bigman said mildly, "Your man was heavier. Your man had experience and still you couldn't leave it a fair fight. You don't take *any* chances, do you? Drop what you're holding . . . Don't the rest of you move, though. From here on in, it's a fair fight in the corridor. No one's moving until someone climbs out of the corridor."

He paused and glared as his fist with the needle-gun moved slowly from side to side. *"But* if it's your ball of gristle that comes back, I'll just be a bit disappointed. And when I'm disappointed, there's no telling what I'll do. I just might be disappointed and mad enough to fire this needle-gun into the crowd, and there isn't a thing in the world any of you can do to stop me from clenching my fist ten times. So if there are ten of you bored with living, just hope that your boy beats Lucky Starr."

Bigman waited there desperately, his right hand holding the needle-gun, his left arm crooked over the V-frog in its container. He longed to order Summers to bring the two men back, to end the fight, but he dared not risk Lucky's anger. He knew Lucky well enough to know that the fight couldn't be allowed to end by default on Lucky's side.

A figure whizzed past the line of sight, then another. There was a crash as of a body hitting a wall, then a second and a third. Then silence.

A figure drifted back, with a second gripped firmly by one ankle.

The person in control came lightly out into the corridor; the person being held followed and dropped like a sack of sand.

Bigman let out a shout. The man standing was Lucky. His cheek was bruised and he limped, but it was Armand who was unconscious.

They brought Armand back to consciousness with some difficulty. He had a lump on his skull resembling a small grapefruit, and one eye was swollen closed. Though his lower lip was bleeding, he managed a painful smile and said, "By Jupiter, this kid's a wildcat."

He got to his feet and threw his arms about Lucky in a bear hug. "It was like tangling with ten men after he got his bearings. He's all right."

Surprisingly, the men were cheering wildly. The V-frog transmitted relief first, swallowed up at once by excitement.

Armand's smile widened, and he dabbed at the blood with the back of his hand. "This councilman is all right. Anyone who still doesn't like him has to fight me, too. Where's Red?"

But Red Summers was gone. So was the instrument he had dropped at Bigman's order.

Armand said, "Listen, Mr. Starr, I've got to tell you. This wasn't my idea, but Red said we had to get rid of you or you'd make trouble for all of us."

Lucky raised his hand. "That's a mistake. Listen, all of you. There'll be no trouble for any loyal Earthman. I guarantee it. This fight is off the record. It was a bit of excitement, but we can forget it. Next time we meet, we all meet fresh. Nothing's happened. Right?"

They cheered madly and there were shouts of "He's all right" and "Up the Council!"

Lucky was turning to go when Armand said, "Hey, wait." He drew in a vast breath and pointed a thick finger. "What's this?" He was pointing to the V-frog.

"A Venusian animal," said Lucky. "A pet of ours."

"It's cute." The giant simpered down at it. The others crowded close to stare at it and make appreciative comments, to seize Lucky's hand and assure him that they had been on his side all along.

Bigman, outraged at the shoving, finally yelled, "Let's get to quarters, Lucky, or I swear I'll kill a few of these guys."

There was an instant silence and men squeezed back to make a path for Lucky and Bigman.

Lucky winced as Bigman applied cold water to the bruised cheek in the privacy of their quarters.

He said, "Some of the men were saying something about needle-guns in that final crush, but in the confusion I didn't get the story straight. Suppose you tell me, Bigman."

Reluctantly Bigman explained the circumstances.

Lucky said thoughtfully, "I realized that my controls were off, but I assumed mechanical failure particularly since they came back after my second fall. I didn't know you and Red Summers were fighting it out over me."

Bigman grinned. "Space, Lucky, you didn't think I'd let that character pull a trick like that?"

"There might have been some way other than needle-guns."

"Nothing else would have frozen them so," said Bigman, aggrieved. "Did you want me to shake my finger at them and say, 'Naughty, naughty?' Besides, I *had* to scare the green bejeebies out of them."

"Why?" Lucky said sharply.

"Sands of Mars, Lucky, you spotted the other guy two falls when the fighting was fixed, and I didn't know if you had enough left to make out. I was going to make Summers call the fight off."

"That would have been bad, Bigman. We would have gained nothing. There would have been men convinced the cry of 'foul' was an unsportsmanlike fake."

"I knew you'd figure that, but I was nervous."

"No need to be. After my controls started responding properly, things went fairly well. Armand was certain he had me, and when he found there was still fight in me, the fight seemed to go out of him. That happens sometimes with people who have never had to lose.

When they don't win at once, it confuses them, and they don't win at all."

"Yes, Lucky," said Bigman, grinning.

Lucky was silent for a minute or two, then he said, "I don't like that 'Yes, Lucky.' What did you do?"

"Well—" Bigman applied the final touch of flesh tint to hide the bruise and stepped back to consider his handiwork critically—"I couldn't help but hope that you'd win, now could I?"

"No, I suppose not."

"And I told everyone in that place that if Armand won, I would shoot as many of them as I could."

"You weren't serious."

"Maybe I was. Anyway, they thought I was; they were sure I was after they saw me needle four buttons off that cobber's shirt. So there were fifty guys there, even including Summers, who were sweating themselves blind hoping you would win and Armand lose."

Lucky said, "So that's it."

"Well, I couldn't help it if the V-frog was there and transmitted all those thoughts to you too, could I?"

"So all the fight went out of Armand because his mind was blanketed with wishes he would lose." Lucky looked chagrined.

"Remember, Lucky. Two foul falls. It wasn't a fair fight."

"Yes, I know. Well, maybe I needed the help at that."

The door signal flashed at that moment, and Lucky raised his eyebrows. "Who's this, I wonder?" He pressed the button that retracted the door into its slot.

A chunky man, with thinning hair and china-blue

eyes that stared at them unblinkingly, stood in the doorway. In one hand he held an oddly shaped piece of
gleaming metal, which his limber fingers turned end
for end. Occasionally the piece ducked between fingers,
traveling from thumb to pinkie and back as though it
had a life of its own. Bigman found himself watching it,
fascinated.

The man said, "My name is Harry Norrich. I'm your
next-door neighbor."

"Good day," said Lucky.

"You're Lucky Starr and Bigman Jones, aren't you?
Would you care to come to my place a few minutes?
Visit a bit, have a drink?"

"That's kind of you," said Lucky. "We'll be glad to
join you."

Norrich turned somewhat stiffly and led the way
down the corridor to the next door. One hand touched
the corridor wall occasionally. Lucky and Bigman followed, the latter holding the V-frog.

"Won't you come in, gentlemen?" He stood aside to
let them enter. "Please sit down. I've heard a great deal
about you already."

"Like what?" asked Bigman.

"Like Lucky's fight with Big Armand and Bigman's
marksmanship with a needle-gun. It's all over the place.
I doubt there's anyone on Jupiter Nine who won't hear
of it by morning. It's one of the reasons I asked you in.
I wanted to talk to you about it."

He poured a reddish liquor carefully into two small
glasses and offered them. For a moment Lucky put his
hand some three inches to one side of the glass, waited
without result, then reached over and took it from
Norrich's hand. Lucky put the drink to one side.

"What's that on your worktable?" asked Bigman.

Norrich's room, in addition to the usual furnishings, had something that looked like a worktable running the length of one wall with a bench before it. On the worktable was a series of metal gimmicks spread out loosely, and in the center was an odd structure, six inches high and very uneven in outline.

"This thing?" Norrich's hand slid delicately along the surface of the table and came to rest on the structure. "It's a threedee."

"A what?"

"A three-dimensional jigsaw. The Japanese had them for thousands of years, but they've never caught on elsewhere. They're puzzles, made up of a number of pieces that fit together to form some sort of structure. This one, for instance, will be the model of an Agrav generator when it's finished. I designed and made this puzzle myself."

He lifted the piece of metal he was holding and placed it carefully in a little slot in the structure. The piece slid in smoothly and held in place.

"Now you take another piece." His left hand moved gently over the structure, while his right felt among the loose pieces, came up with one, and moved it into place.

Bigman, fascinated, moved forward, then jumped back at a sudden animal howl from beneath the table.

A dog came squirming out from beneath the table and put its forefeet on the bench. It was a large German shepherd dog and it stood now looking mildly at Bigman.

Bigman said nervously, "Here, now, I stepped on it by accident."

"It's only Mutt," said Norrich. "He won't hurt any-one without better cause than being stepped on. He's my dog. He's my eyes."

"Your eyes?"

Lucky said softly, "Mr. Norrich is blind, Bigman."

6

Death Enters the Game

Bigman shrank back. "I'm sorry."

"No need to be sorry," Norrich said cheerfully. "I'm used to it and I can get along. I'm holding a master technician's rank and I'm in charge of constructing experimental jigs. I don't need anyone to help me, either, any more than I need help in my threedees."

"I imagine the threedees offer good exercise," said Lucky.

Bigman said, "You mean you can put those things together without even being able to see them? Sands of Mars!"

"It's not as hard as you might think. I've been practicing for years and I make them myself so I know the tricks of them. Here, Bigman, here's a simple one. It's just an egg shape. Can you take it apart?"

Bigman received the light-alloy ovoid and turned it in his hands, looking over the pieces that fit together smoothly and neatly.

"In fact," Norrich went on, "the only thing I really need Mutt for is to take me along the corridors." He leaned down to scratch the dog behind one ear, and the dog permitted it, opening his mouth wide in a sleepy yawn, showing large white fangs and a length of pink lolling tongue. Lucky could feel the warm thickness of Norrich's affection for the dog pour out via the V-frog.

"I can't use the Agrav corridors," Norrich said, "since I'd have no way of telling when to decelerate, so I have to walk through ordinary corridors and Mutt guides me. It makes for the long way around, but it's good exercise, and with all the walking Mutt and I know Jupiter Nine better than anybody, don't we, Mutt? . . . Have you got it yet, Bigman?"

"No," said Bigman. "It's all one piece."

"Not really. Here, give it to me."

Bigman handed it over, and Norrich's skillful fingers flew over the surface. "See this little square bit here? You push it and it goes in a bit. Grab the part that comes out the other end, give it half a turn clockwise, and it pulls out altogether. See? Now the rest comes apart easily. This, then this, then this, and so on. Line up the pieces in order as they come out; there are only eight of them; then put them back in reverse order. Put the key piece in last, and it will lock everything into place."

Bigman stared dubiously at the individual pieces and bent close over them.

Lucky said, "I believe you wanted to discuss the reception committee I met up with when I arrived, Mr. Norrich. You said you wanted to talk about my fight with Armand."

"Yes, Councilman, yes. I wanted you to understand. I've been here on Jupiter Nine since Agrav project started and I know the men. Some leave when their hitch is up, some stay on, greenhorns join up; but they're all the same in one way. They're very insecure."

"Why?"

"For several reasons. In the first place, there is danger involved in the project. We've had dozens of accidents and lost hundreds of men. I lost my eyes five years ago and I was fortunate in a way. I might have died. Secondly, the men are isolated from friends and family while they're here. Really isolated."

Lucky said, "I imagine there are some people who enjoy the isolation."

He smiled grimly as he said that. It was no secret that men who in one way or another had gotten entangled with the law sometimes managed to find work on some of the pioneer worlds. People were always needed to work under domes in artificial atmospheres with pseudo-grav fields, and those who volunteered were usually not asked too many questions. Nor was there anything very wrong with that. Such volunteers aided Earth and its people under difficult conditions, and that, in a way, was a payment for misdeeds.

Norrich nodded at Lucky's words. "I see you're not naïve about it and I'm glad. Leaving the officers and the professional engineers to one side, I imagine a good half of the men here have criminal records on Earth, and most of the rest might have such records if the police knew everything. I doubt that one in five gives his real name. Anyway, you see where tension comes in when investigator after investigator arrives. You're all looking for Sirian spies; we know that; but each man thinks that maybe his own particular trouble will come out and he'll be dragged back to jail on Earth. They all want to go back to Earth, but they want to go back anonymously, not at the other end of a set of wrist locks. That's why Red Summers could rouse them so."

"And is Summers something special that he takes the lead? A particularly bad record on Earth?"

Bigman looked up briefly from his threedee to say bitterly, "Murder, maybe?"

"No," said Norrich with instant energy. "You've got to understand about Summers. He's had an unfortunate life: broken home, no real parents. He got into the wrong crowds. He's been in prison, yes, for being involved in some minor rackets. If he'd stayed on Earth, his life would have been one long waste. But he's come to Jupiter Nine. He's made a new life here. He came out as a common laborer and he educated himself. He's learned low-grav construction engineering, force-field mechanics, and Agrav techniques. He's been promoted to a responsible position and has done wonderful work. He's respectable, admired, well liked. He's found out what it is to have honor and position and he dreads nothing more than the thought of going back to Earth and his old life."

"Sure, he hates it so much," said Bigman, "that he tried to kill Lucky by gimmicking the fight."

"Yes," said Norrich, frowning, "I heard he was using a sub-phase oscillator to kill the councilman's control response. That was stupid of him, but he was in panic. Look, fundamentally the man is goodhearted. When my old Mutt died—"

"Your old Mutt?" asked Lucky.

"I had a Seeing Eye dog before this one which I also called Mutt. It died in a force-field short circuit that killed two men besides. He shouldn't have been there, but sometimes a dog will wander off on his own adventures. This one does, too, when I'm not using him, but he always comes back." He leaned down to slap his dog's flank lightly, and Mutt closed one eye and thumped his tail against the floor.

"Anyway, after old Mutt died, it looked for a while as though I mightn't get another and I would have to be sent home. I'm no use here without one. Seeing Eye dogs are in short supply; there are waiting lists. The administration here at Jupiter Nine didn't want to pull any strings because they weren't anxious to publicize the fact that they were employing a blind man as construction engineer. The economy bloc in Congress is always waiting for something like that to make bad publicity out of. So it was Summers who came through. He used some contacts he had on Earth and got me Mutt here. It wasn't exactly legal, it was even what you might call the black market, but Summers risked his position here to do a friend a favor and I owe him a great deal. I'm hoping you'll remember Summers can do and has done things like that and that you'll go easy on him for his actions earlier today."

Lucky said, "I'm not taking any action against him. I had no intention of doing so even before our conversation. Still, I'm sure that Summers' real name and record are known to the Council and I'll be checking on the facts."

Norrich flushed, "By all means, do so. You'll find he's not so bad."

"I hope so. But tell me something. Through all that has just taken place, there was no attempt on the part of the project administration to interfere. Do you find this strange?"

Norrich laughed shortly. "Not at all. I don't think Commander Donahue would have cared much if you'd been killed, except for the trouble it would have taken to hush it up. He's got bigger troubles on his mind than you or your investigation."

"Bigger troubles?"

"Sure. The head of this project is changed every year; army policy of rotation. Donahue is the sixth boss we've had and far and away the best. I've got to say that. He's cut through red tape and he hasn't tried to make an army camp out of the project. He's given the men leeway and let them raise a bit of cain now and then so he's gotten results. Now the first Agrav ship will be ready to take off any time. Some say it's a matter of days."

"That soon?"

"Could be. But the point is that Commander Donahue is due to be relieved in less than a month. A delay now could mean that the launching of the Agrav ship won't take place until Donahue's successor comes in. Donahue's successor would get to ride in it, have the fame, go down in the history books, and Donahue would miss out."

"No wonder he didn't want you on Jupiter Nine," Bigman said hotly. "No wonder he didn't want you, Lucky."

Lucky shrugged. "Don't waste temper, Bigman."

But Bigman said, "The dirty cobber! Sirius can gobble up Earth for all he cares as long as he can get to ride his miserable ship." He lifted a clenched fist, and there was a muted growl from Mutt.

Norrich said sharply, "What are you doing, Bigman?"

"What?" Bigman was genuinely astonished. "I'm not doing a thing."

"Are you making a threatening gesture?"

Bigman lowered his arm quickly. "Not really."

"You've got to be careful around Mutt. He's been trained to take care of me. . . . Look, I'll show you. Just step toward me and make believe you're going to throw a punch at me."

Lucky said, "That's not necessary. We understand—"

"Please," said Norrich. "There's no danger. I'll stop Mutt in time. As a matter of fact, it's good practice for him. Everyone on the project is so careful of me that I swear I don't know if he remembers his training. Go ahead, Bigman."

Bigman stepped forward and raised his arm half-heartedly. At once Mutt's ears flattened, his eyes slitted, his fangs stood sharply revealed, his leg muscles tensed for a spring, and a harsh growl issued from the recesses of his throat.

Bigman drew back hastily, and Norrich said, "Down, Mutt!" The dog subsided. Lucky could sense, clearly, the gathering and relaxation of tension in Bigman's mind and the fond triumph in Norrich's.

Norrish said, "How are you doing with the threedee egg, Bigman?"

The little Martian, in exasperation, said, "I've given up. I've got two pieces put together and that's all I can do."

Norrich laughed. "Just a matter of practice, that's all. Look."

He took the two pieces out of Bigman's hand and said, "No wonder. You've got these together wrong. He flipped one piece end for end, brought the two together again, added another piece and another until he

held seven pieces in the shape of a loose ovoid with a
hole through it. He picked up the eighth and key piece,
slipped it in, gave it a half turn counterclockwise,
pushed it the rest of the way, and said, "Finished."

He tossed the completed egg into the air and caught
it, while Bigman watched in chagrin.

Lucky got to his feet. "Well, Mr. Norrich, we'll be
seeing you again. I'll remember your remarks about
Summers and the rest. Thank you for the drink." It
still rested untouched on the desk.

"Nice to have met you," said Norrich, rising and
shaking hands.

It was some time before Lucky could fall asleep. He
lay in the darkness of his room hundreds of feet below
the surface of Jupiter Nine, listening to Bigman's soft
snoring in the adjoining room, and thought of the
events of the day. Over and over them he went.

He was bothered! Something had happened that
shouldn't have; or something had not happened that
should have.

But he was weary and everything was a bit unreal and
twisted in the half-world of half-sleep. Something hovered at the edge of awareness. He clutched at it, but it
slipped away.

And when morning came there was nothing left of it.

Bigman called out to Lucky from his own room as
Lucky was drying himself under the soft jets of warm
air after his shower.

The little Martian yelled, "Hey, Lucky, I've re-
charged the V-frog's carbon-dioxide supply and dumped
in more weed. You'll be taking it down to our meeting
with that blasted commander, won't you?"

"We certainly will, Bigman."

"It's all set then. How about letting me tell the commander what I think of him?"

"Now, Bigman."

"Nuts! It's me for the shower now."

Like all men of the solar system brought up on planets other than Earth, Bigman reveled in water when he could get at it, and a shower for him was a leisurely, loving experience. Lucky braced himself for a session of the tenor caterwauling that Bigman called singing.

The intercom sounded after Bigman was well launched into some dubious fragment of melody that sounded piercingly off-key and just as Lucky completed dressing.

Lucky stepped to it and activated reception. "Starr speaking."

"Starr!" Commander Donahue's lined face showed in the visi-panel. His lips were narrow and compressed and his whole expression was one of antagonism as he gazed at Lucky. "I have heard some story of a fight between yourself and one of our workers."

"Yes?"

"I see you have not been hurt."

Lucky smiled. "All's well."

"You'll remember I warned you."

"I am making no complaints."

"Since you aren't, and in the interest of the project, I would like to ask if you plan making any report concerning it."

"Unless it turns out to have some direct bearing on the problem which concerns me here, the incident will never be mentioned by me."

"Good!" Donahue looked suddenly relieved. "I won-

der if I could. extend that attitude to our meeting this
morning. Our meeting might be taped for confidential
records and I would prefer—"

"There will be no need to discuss the matter, Commander."

"Very good!" The commander relaxed into what was
almost cordiality. "I'll be seeing you in an hour then."

Lucky was dimly aware that Bigman's shower had
stopped and that his singing had subsided to a humming. Now the humming stopped, too, and there was
a moment of silence.

Lucky said into the transmitter, "Yes, Commander,
good—" when Bigman exploded into a wild, near-
incoherent shout.

"Lucky!"

Lucky was on his feet with smooth speed and at the
door connecting the two rooms in two strides.

But Bigman was in the doorway before him, eyes big
with horror. "Lucky! The V-frog! It's dead! It's been
killed!"

7

A Robot Enters the Game

The V-frog's plastic cage was shattered and shriveled, and the floor was wet with its watery contents. The V-frog, half covered with the fronds it fed upon, was quite, quite dead.

Now that it was dead and unable to control emotion, Lucky could look at it without the enforced fondness that he, as well as all others that came within its radius of influence, had felt. He felt anger, however—mostly at himself for having allowed himself to be overreached.

Bigman, fresh from his shower, with only his shorts on, clenched and unclenched his fists. "It's my fault, Lucky. It's all my fault. I was yelling so loud in the shower I never heard anyone come in."

The phrase "come in" was not quite appropriate. The killer had not simply come in; he had burnt his way in. The lock controls were fused and melted away with what had obviously been an energy projector of fairly large caliber.

Lucky stepped back to the interphone. "Commander Donahue?"

"Yes, what happened? Is anything wrong?"

"I'll see you in an hour." He broke connections and returned to the grieving Bigman. He said somberly, "It's my fault, Bigman. Uncle Hector said the Sirians had not yet discovered the facts concerning the emotional powers of the V-frog, and I accepted that too thoroughly. If I had been a little less optimistic about Sirian ignorance, neither one of us would ever have left that little creature out of our sight for a second."

Lieutenant Nevsky called for them, standing at attention as Lucky and Bigman left their quarters.

He said in a low voice, "I am glad, sir, that you were unharmed in yesterday's encounter. I would not have left you, sir, had you not strictly ordered me to."

"Forget it, Lieutenant," Lucky said absently. His mind kept returning to that moment just before sleep the preceding night when, for a brief instant, a thought had hovered at the outskirts of consciousness, then vanished. But it would not come now, and finally Lucky's mind sped to other matters.

They had entered the Agrav corridor now, and this time it seemed crowded with men, streaming accurately and unconcernedly in both directions. There was a "beginning of the work day" atmosphere all about. Though men worked underground here and there was no day or night, yet the old twenty-four-hour schedule held. Mankind brought the familiar rotation of the Earth to all the worlds on which he lived. And though men might work in shifts the clock round, the largest number always worked on the "day shift" from nine to five, Solar Standard Time.

It was nearly nine now, and there was a bustle

through the Agrav corridors as men traveled to the work posts. There was a feel of "morning" almost as strong as though there were a sun low in the eastern sky and dew on the grass.

Two men were sitting at the table when Lucky and Bigman entered the conference room. One was Commander Donahue, whose face bore the appearance of a carefully controlled tension. The commander rose and coldly introduced the other: James Panner, the chief engineer and civilian head of the project. Panner was a stocky man with a swarthy face, dark deep-set eyes, and a bull neck. He wore a dark shirt open at the collar and without insignia of any sort.

Lieutenant Nevsky saluted and retired. Commander Donahue watched the door close and said, "Since that leaves the four of us, let's get to business."

"The four of us and a cat," said Lucky, stroking a small creature that hitched its forepaws on the table and stared at him solemnly. "This isn't the same cat I saw yesterday, is it?"

The commander frowned. "Perhaps. Perhaps not. We have a number of cats on the satellite. However, I presume we're not here to discuss pets."

Lucky said, "On the contrary, Commander, I think it will do as a topic of conversation to begin with and I chose it deliberately. Do you remember my own pet, sir?"

"Your little Venusian creature?" said the commander with sudden warmth. "I remember it. It was—" He stopped in confusion as though wondering, in the V-frog's absence, what the reason for his enthusiasm concerning it might be.

"The little Venusian creature," said Lucky, "had peculiar abilities. It could detect emotion. It could transmit emotion. It could even impose emotion."

The commander's eyes opened wide, but Panner said in a husky voice, "I once heard a rumor to that effect, Councilman. I laughed."

"You needn't have. It is true. In fact, Commander Donahue, my purpose in asking for this interview was to make arrangements to have every man on the project interviewed by me in the presence of the V-frog. I wanted an emotional analysis."

The commander still seemed half stunned. "What would that prove?"

"Perhaps nothing. Still, I meant to try it."

Panner intervened. *"Meant* to try it? You use the past tense, Councilman Starr."

Lucky stared solemnly at the two project officials. "My V-frog is dead."

Bigman said furiously, "Killed this morning."

The commander said, "Who killed it?"

"We don't know, Commander."

The commander sat back in his chair. "Then your little investigation is over, I suppose, till the animal can be replaced."

Lucky said, "There will be no waiting. The mere fact of the V-frog's death has told me a great deal, and the matter becomes much more serious."

"What do you mean?"

All stared. Even Bigman looked up at Lucky in profound surprise.

Lucky said, "I told you that the V-frog has the capacity to impose emotion. You yourself, Commander Donahue, experienced that. Do you recall your feelings when you saw the V-frog on my ship yesterday? You were under considerable strain, yet when you saw the V-frog— Do you remember your feelings, sir?"

"I was rather taken with the creature," the commander faltered.

"Can you think why, as you look back at the moment now?"

"No, come to think of it. Ugly creature."

"Yet you liked it. You couldn't help yourself. Could you have harmed it?"

"I suppose not."

"I'm certain you couldn't. No one with emotions could have. Yet someone did. Someone killed it."

Panner said, "Do you intend to explain the paradox?"

"Easily explained. No one *with emotions*. A robot, however, does *not* have emotions. Suppose that somewhere on Jupiter Nine there is a robot, a mechanical man, in the perfect form of a human being?"

"You mean a humanoid?" exploded Commander Donahue. "Impossible. Such things exist only in fairy tales."

Lucky said, "I think, Commander, you are not aware of how skillful the Sirians are in the manufacture of robots. I think they might be able to use some man on Jupiter Nine, some thoroughly loyal man, as model; build a robot in his shape and substitute it for him. Such a humanoid robot could have special senses that would enable it to be the perfect spy. It might, for instance, be able to see in the dark or sense things through thicknesses of matter. It would certainly be able to transmit information through the subether by some built-in device."

The commander shook his head. "Ridiculous. A man

could easily have killed the V-frog. A desperate man frightened to an extreme might have overcome this— this mental influence the animal exerted. Have you thought of that?"

"Yes, I have," said Lucky. "But why should a man be so desperate, why so wild to kill a harmless V-frog? The most obvious reason is that the V-frog represented a desperate danger, that it was not harmless at all. The only danger a V-frog might have to the killer would involve the animal's capacity to detect and transmit the killer's emotions. Suppose those emotions would be an immediate giveaway to the fact that the killer was a spy?"

"How could it be?" Panner asked.

Lucky turned to look at him. "What if our killer had no emotions at all? Wouldn't a man without emotions be revealed at once as a robot? . . . Or take it another way altogether. Why kill only the V-frog? Having gotten into our rooms, having risked so much, having found one of us in the shower and one at the intercom and both unsuspecting and unready, why did not the killer kill *us* instead of the V-frog? For that matter, why not kill us *and* the V-frog?"

"No time, probably," said the commander.

"There's another and more plausible reason," said Lucky. "Do you know the Three Laws of Robotics, the rules of behavior that all robots are built to follow?"

"I know them generally," the commander said. "I can't quote them."

"I can," said Lucky, "and with your permission I will, so that I may make a point. The First Law is this: A robot may not injure a human being or, through inaction, allow a human being to come to harm. The

Second Law is: A robot must obey the orders given it by human beings except where such orders would conflict with the First Law. The Third Law is: A robot must protect its own existence as long as such protection does not conflict with the First or Second Law."

Panner nodded. "All right, Councilman, what does that prove?"

"A robot can be ordered to kill the V-frog, which is an animal. It will risk its existence, since self-preservation is only Third Law, to obey orders, which is Second Law. But it cannot be ordered to kill Bigman or myself, since we are humans, and First Law takes precedence over all. A human spy would have killed us and the V-frog; a robot spy would have killed only the V-frog. It all points to the same thing, Commander."

The commander considered that for long minutes, sitting motionless, the lines on his tired face grooving deeper. Then he said, "What do you propose to do? X-ray every man on the project?"

"No," said Lucky at once. "It's not that simple. Successful espionage is going on elsewhere than here. If there is a humanoid robot here, there are probably others elsewhere. It would be well to catch as many of the humanoids as possible; all of them if we can. If we act too eagerly and openly to catch the one under our hands, the others may be snatched away for use at another time."

"Then what *do* you propose doing?"

"To work slowly. Once you suspect a robot, there are ways of making it give itself away without its being aware of it. And I don't start completely from scratch. For instance, Commander, I know you are not a robot, since I detected emotion in you yesterday. In fact, I deliberately induced anger in you to test my V-frog, and for that I ask your pardon."

Donahue's face had gone mauve. "I, a robot?"

"As I said, I used you only to test my V-frog."

Panner said dryly, "You have no reason to feel sure about me, Councilman. I never faced your V-frog."

"That is right," said Lucky. "You are not cleared yet. Remove your shirt."

"What!" cried Panner indignantly. "Why?"

Lucky said mildly, "You have just been cleared. A robot would have had to obey that order."

The commander's fist banged down on his desk. *"Stop it!* This ends right here. I will not have you testing or annoying my men in any way. I have a job to do on this satellite, Councilman Starr; I have an Agrav ship to get into space, and I'm getting it into space. My men have been investigated and they're clear. Your story about a robot is flimsy, and I'm not going along with it.

"I told you yesterday, Starr, that I didn't want you on this satellite disturbing my men and wrecking their morale. You saw fit yesterday to address me in insulting fashion. You say now it was just to test your animal, which makes it no less insulting. For that reason, I feel no need to co-operate with you and I am not doing so. Let me tell you exactly what I have done.

"I've cut off all communication with Earth. I've put Jupiter Nine under emergency orders. I have the powers of a military dictator now. Do you understand?"

Lucky's eyes narrowed a trifle. "As councilman of the Council of Science, I outrank you."

"How do you intend to enforce your rank? My men

will obey me and they have their orders. You will be restrained forcibly if you try in any way, by word or deed, to interfere with my orders."

"And what are your orders?"

"Tomorrow," said Commander Donahue, "at 6 P.M., Solar Standard Time, the first functioning Agrav ship in existence will make its first flight from Jupiter Nine to Jupiter One, the satellite Io. After we're back— *after* we're back, Councilman Starr, and not one hour sooner—you may conduct your investigation. And if you then want to get in touch with Earth and arrange court-martial proceedings, I will be ready for you."

Commander Donahue stared firmly at Lucky Starr.

Lucky said to Panner, "Is the ship ready?"

Panner said, "I think so."

Donahue said scornfully. "We leave tomorrow. Well, Councilman Starr, do you go along with me or will I have to have you arrested?"

The silence that followed was a tense one. Bigman virtually held his breath. The commander's hands were clenching and unclenching, and his nose was white and pinched. Panner slowly fumbled a stick of gum out of his shirt pocket, stripped it of its plastofoil coating with one hand, and crumpled it into his mouth.

And then Lucky clasped his hands loosely, sat back in his chair, and said, "I'll be glad to co-operate with you, Commander."

8

Blindness

Bigman was at once outraged. "Lucky! Are you going to let him stop the investigation just like that?"

Lucky said, "Not exactly, Bigman. We'll be on board the Agrav ship and we'll continue it there."

"No sir," the commander said flatly, "You will not be on board. Don't think that for an instant."

Lucky said, "Who will be on board, Commander? Yourself, I presume?"

"Myself. Also Panner, as chief engineer. Two of my officers, five other engineers, and five ordinary crewmen. All these were chosen some time ago. Myself and Panner, as responsible heads of the project; the five engineers to handle the ship itself; the remainder in return for their services to the project."

Lucky said thoughtfully, "What type of service?"

Panner interrupted to say, "The best example of what the commander is talking about is Harry Norrich, who—"

Bigman stiffened in surprise. "You mean the blind fellow?"

Panner said, "You know him then?"

"We met him last evening," said Lucky.

"Well," said Panner, "Norrich was here at the very beginning of the project. He lost his sight when he threw himself between two contacts to keep a force field from buckling. He was in the hospital five months and his eyes were the one part of him that couldn't be restored. By his act of bravery, he kept the satellite from having a chunk the size of a mountain blown out of it. He saved the lives of two hundred people *and* he saved the project, since a major accident at the beginning might have made it impossible to get further appropriations out of Congress. That sort of thing is what earns one the honor of a place on the maiden voyage of the Agrav ship."

"It's a shame he won't be able to see Jupiter up close," said Bigman. Then, his eyes narrowing, "How'll he get around on board ship?"

Panner said, "We'll be taking Mutt, I'm sure. He's a well-behaved dog."

"That's all I want to know then," said Bigman heatedly. "If you cobbers can take a dog, you can take Lucky and me."

Commander Donahue was looking at his wristwatch impatiently. Now he put the palms of his hands flat on the table and made as though to rise. "We have finished our business then, gentlemen."

"Not quite," Lucky said. "There's one little point to be cleared up. Bigman puts it crudely, but he's quite right. He and I will be on the Agrav ship when it leaves."

"No," said Commander Donahue. "Impossible."

"Is the added mass of two individuals too great for the ship to handle?"

Panner laughed. "We could move a mountain."

"Do you lack room then?"

The commander stared at Lucky in hard displeasure. "I will not give any reason. You are not being taken only because it is my decision that you not be taken. Is that clear?"

There was a glint of satisfaction in his eyes, and Lucky did not find it hard to guess that he was squaring accounts for the tongue-lashing Lucky had given him aboard the *Lucky Starr*.

Lucky said quietly, "You had better take us, Commander."

Donahue smiled sardonically. "Why? Am I to be relieved of duty at the orders of the Council of Science? You won't be able to communicate with Earth till I return, and after that they can relieve me of duty if they wish."

"I don't think you've thought it through, Commander," said Lucky. "They might relieve you of duty retroactive to this moment. In fact, I assure you they will do so. As far as the government records are concerned, then, it will appear that Agrav ship made its first flight not under your command but under the command, officially, of your successor, whoever he might be. The records of the trip might even be adjusted to show, officially, that you were not on board."

Commander Donahue went white. He rose and for a moment seemed on the point of throwing himself bodily at Lucky.

Lucky said, "Your decision, Commander?"

Donahue's voice was most unnatural when it finally came. "You may come."

Lucky spent the remainder of the day in the record rooms, studying the files on various men employed on the project, while Bigman, under Panner's guidance, was taken from laboratory to laboratory and through tremendous testing rooms.

It was only after the evening meal when they returned to quarters that they had a chance to be alone together. Lucky's silence then was not extraordinary, since the young councilman was never talkative at the best of times, but there was a small crease between his eyes that Bigman recognized as a sure sign of concern.

Bigman said, "We aren't making any progress, are we, Lucky?"

Lucky shook his head, "Nothing startling, I'll admit."

He had brought a book-film with him from the project's library, and Bigman caught a flash of its title: *Advanced Robotics*. Methodically Lucky threaded the beginnings of the film through the viewer.

Bigman stirred restlessly. "Are you going to be all tied up with that film, Lucky?"

"I'm afraid so, Bigman."

"Do you mind then if I visit Norrich next door for company?"

"Go ahead." Lucky had the viewer over his eyes and he was leaning back, his arms crossed loosely across his chest.

Bigman closed the door and remained standing just outside for a moment, a little nervous. He should discuss this with Lucky first, he knew he should, and yet the temptation . . .

He told himself: I'm not going to do anything. I'll just check something. If I'm wrong, I'm wrong and why bother Lucky? But if it checks out, then I'll *really* have something to tell him.

The door opened at once when he rang, and there was Norrich, blind eyes fixed in the direction of the doorway, seated before a desk on which a checkerboard design carried odd figures.

He said, "Yes?"

"This is Bigman," said the little Martian.

"Bigman! Come in. Sit down. Is Councilman Starr with you?"

The door closed again, and Bigman looked about in the brightly lit room. His mouth tightened. "He's busy. But as for me, I'm filled up on Agrav today. Dr. Panner took me all over, only I don't understand a thing of it hardly."

Norrich smiled. "You're not exactly in a minority, but if you ignore the mathematics, some of it isn't too hard to understand."

"No? Mind explaining it then?" Bigman sat down in a large chair and bent to look under Norrich's workbench. Mutt lay there with his head between his forepaws and one eye brightly fixed on Bigman.

(Keep him talking, thought Bigman. Keep him talking till I find a hole, or make one.)

"Look here," Norrich said. He held up one of the round counters he had been holding. "Gravity is a form of energy. An object such as this piece I'm holding which is under the influence of a gravitational field but is not allowed to move is said to have potential energy. If I were to release the piece, that potential energy would be converted to motion—or kinetic energy, as it is called. Since it continues under the influence of the gravitational field as it falls, it falls faster and faster and faster." He dropped the counter at this point, and it fell.

"Until, splash," said Bigman. The counter hit the floor and rolled.

Norrich bent as though to retrieve it and then said, "Would you get it for me, Bigman? I'm not sure where it rolled."

Bigman suppressed his disappointment. He picked it up and returned it.

Norrich said, "Now until recently that was the only thing that could be done with potential energy: it could be converted into kinetic energy. Of course the kinetic energy could be used further. For instance, the falling water of Niagara Falls could be used to form electricity, but that's a different thing. In space, gravity results in motion and that ends it.

"Consider the Jovian system of moons. We're at Jupiter Nine, way out. Fifteen million miles out. With respect to Jupiter, we've got a tremendous quantity of potential energy. If we try to travel to Jupiter One, the satellite Io, which is only 285,000 miles from Jupiter, we are in a way, falling all those millions of miles. We pick up tremendous speeds which we must continually counteract by pushing in the opposite direction with a hyperatomic motor. It takes enormous energy. Then, if we miss our mark by a bit, we're in constant danger of continuing to fall, in which case there's only one place to go, and that's Jupiter—and Jupiter is instant death. *Then,* even if we land safely on Io, there's the problem of getting back to Jupiter Nine, which means lifting ourselves all those millions of miles against Jupiter's gravity. The amount of energy required to maneuver among Jupiter's moons is just prohibitive."

"And Agrav?" asked Bigman.

"Ah! Now that's a different thing. Once you use an Agrav converter, potential energy can be converted into forms of energy *other* than kinetic energy. In the Agrav corridor, for instance, the force of gravity in one direction is used to charge the gravitational field in the other direction as you fall. People falling in one direction provide the energy for people falling in the other. By bleeding off the energy that way, you yourself, while falling, need never speed up. You can fall at any velocity less than the natural falling velocity. You see?"

Bigman wasn't quite sure he did but he said, "Go on."

"In space it's different. There's no second gravitational field to shift the energy to. Instead, it is converted to hyperatomic field energy and stored so. By doing this, a space ship can drop from Jupiter Nine to Io at any speed less than the natural falling speed without having to use any energy to decelerate. Virtually no energy is expended except in the final adjustment to Io's orbital speed. And safety is complete, since the ship is always under perfect control. Jupiter's gravity could be completely blanketed, if necessary.

"Going back to Jupiter Nine still requires energy. There is no getting around that. But now you can use the energy you had previously stored in the hyperatomic field condenser to get you back. The energy of Jupiter's own gravitational field is used to kick you back."

Bigman said, "It sounds good." He squirmed in his

seat. He wasn't getting anywhere. Suddenly he said, "What's that you're fooling with on your desk?"

"Chess," said Norrich. "Do you play?"

"A little," Bigman confessed. "Lucky taught me, but it's no fun playing with him. He always wins." Then he asked, offhand, "How can *you* play chess?"

"You mean because I'm blind?"

"Uh—"

"It's all right. I'm not sensitive about being blind. . . . It's easy enough to explain. This board is magnetized and the pieces are made of a light magnetic alloy so that they stick where they're put and don't go tumbling if I move my arm about carelessly. Here, try it, Bigman."

Bigman reached for one of the pieces. It came up as though stuck in syrup for a quarter of an inch or so, then was free.

"And you see," said Norrich, "they're not ordinary chess pieces."

"More like checkers," grunted Bigman.

"Again so I don't knock them over. They're not completely flat, though. They've got raised designs which I can identify easily enough by touch and which resemble the ordinary pieces closely enough so that other people can learn them in a moment and play with me. See for yourself."

Bigman had no trouble. The circle of raised points was obviously the queen, while the little cross in the center of another piece signified the king. The pieces with grooves slanting across were the bishops, the raised circle of squares the rooks, the pointed horse's ears the knights, and the simple round knobs the pawns.

Bigman felt stymied. He said, "What are you doing now? Playing a game by yourself?"

"No, solving a problem. The pieces are arranged just so, you see, and there's one way and only one in which white can win the game in exactly three moves and I'm trying to find that way."

Bigman said suddenly, "How can you tell white from black?"

Norrich laughed. "If you'll look closely, you'll see the white pieces are grooved along the rims and the black pieces aren't."

"Oh. Then you have to remember where all the pieces are, don't you?"

"That's not hard," Norrich said. "It sounds as though you would need a photographic memory, but actually all I have to do is pass my hand over the board and check the pieces any time. You'll notice the squares are marked off by little grooves, too."

Bigman found himself breathing hard. He had forgotten about the squares on the checkerboard, and they *were* grooved off. He felt as though he were playing a kind of a chess game of his own, one in which he was being badly beaten.

"Mind if I watch?" he said sharply. "Maybe I can figure out the right moves."

"By all means," said Norrich. "I wish you could. I've been at this for half an hour and I'm getting frustrated."

There was silence for a minute or more, and then Bigman rose, his body tense and catlike in its effort to make no noise. He drew a small flashlight from one pocket and stepped toward the wall in little motions. Norrich never moved from his bowed position over the chessboard. Bigman threw a quick glance toward Mutt, but the dog made no move, either.

Bigman reached the wall and, hardly breathing, put one hand lightly and noiselessly over the light patch. At once, the light in the room went out and a profound darkness rested everywhere.

Bigman remembered the direction in which Norrich's chair was. He raised the flashlight.

He heard a muted thump and then Norrich's voice calling out in surprise and a little displeasure, "Why did you put out the light, Bigman?"

"That does it," yelled Bigman in triumph. He let the flashlight's beam shine full on Norrich's broad face. "You're not blind at all, you spy."

9

The Agrav Ship

Norrich cried out, "I don't know what you're doing, but Space, man, don't do anything sudden or Mutt will jump you!"

"You know exactly what I'm doing," said Bigman, "because you can see well enough I'm drawing my needle-gun, and I think you've heard I'm a dead shot. If your dog moves in my direction, it's the end for him."

"Don't hurt Mutt. Please!"

Bigman was taken aback by the sudden anguish in the other's voice. He said, "Just keep him quiet then and come with me and no one will be hurt. We'll go see Lucky. And if we pass anyone in the corridor, don't you say anything but 'Good day.' I'll be right beside you, you know."

Norrich said, "I can't go without Mutt."

"Sure you can," said Bigman. "It's only five steps down the corridor. Even if you were really blind, you could manage that—a fellow who can do threedees and all."

Lucky lifted the viewer from his head at the sound of

the door opening and said, "Good day, Norrich. Where's Mutt?"

Bigman spoke before the other had a chance to answer. "Mutt's in Norrich's room, and Norrich doesn't need him. Sands of Mars. Lucky, Norrich isn't any blinder than we are!"

"What?"

Norrich began, "Your friend is quite mistaken, Mr. Starr. I want to say——"

Bigman snapped. "Quiet, you! I'll talk, and then when you're invited, you can make some remarks."

Lucky folded his arms. "If you don't mind, Mr. Norrich, I'd like to hear what Bigman has on his mind. And meanwhile, Bigman, suppose you put away the needle-gun."

Bigman did so with a grimace. He said, "Look, Lucky, I suspected this cobber from the beginning. Those threedee puzzles of his set me to thinking. He was just a little too good. I got to wondering right away that he might be the spy."

"That's the second time you've called me a spy," Norrich cried. "I won't stand for that."

"Look, Lucky," said Bigman, ignoring Norrich's outcry, "it would be a clever move to have a spy a supposed blind man. He could see an awful lot no one would think he was seeing. People wouldn't cover up. They wouldn't hide things. He could be staring right at some vital document and they'd think, 'It's only poor Norrich. He can't see.' More likely they wouldn't give it a thought at all. Sands of Mars, it would be a perfect setup!"

Norrich was looking more astonished with every

moment. "But I *am* blind. If it's the threedee puzzles or the chess, I've explained—"

"Oh, sure, you've explained," Bigman said scornfully. "You've been practicing explanations for years. How come you sit in the privacy of your room with the lights on, though? When I walked in, Lucky, about half an hour ago, the light was on. He hadn't just put it on for me. The switch was too far away from where he was sitting. Why?"

"Why not?" said Norrich. "It makes no difference to me whether it's on or not, so it might as well be on as long as I'm awake for the convenience of those who come visiting, like you."

"All right," said Bigman. "That shows how he can think up an explanation for everything—how he can play chess, how he can identify the pieces, everything. Once he almost forgot himself. He dropped one of his chess pieces and bent to pick it up when he remembered just in time and asked me to do it for him."

"Usually," said Norrich, "I can tell where something drops by the sound. This piece rolled."

"Go on, explain," said Bigman. "It won't help you because there's one thing you *can't* explain. Lucky, I was going to test him. I was going to put out the light, then flash my pocketlight in his eyes at full intensity. If he weren't blind, he'd be bound to jump or blink his eyes anyway. I was sure I'd get him. But I didn't even have to go that far. As soon as I put out the light, the poor cobber forgets himself and says, 'Why did you put out the light?' . . . How did he know I put out the light, Lucky? *How did he know?*"

"But—" Norrich began.

Bigman drove on. "He can feel chess pieces and

threedee puzzles and all that but he can't feel light going out. He had to *see* that."

Lucky said, "I think it's time to let Mr. Norrich say something."

Norrich said, "Thank you. I may be blind, Councilman, but my dog is not. When I put out the light at night, it makes no difference to me, as I said before, but to Mutt it signals bedtime and he goes to his own corner. Now I heard Bigman tiptoe to the wall in the direction of the light switch. He was trying to move without sound, but a man who has been blind for five years can hear the lightest tiptoe. A moment after he stopped walking I heard Mutt jump into his corner. It didn't take much brain power to figure out what had happened. Bigman was standing at the light switch and Mutt was turning in for the night. Obviously he had put out the light."

The engineer turned his sightless face in the direction first of Bigman, then of Lucky, as though straining his ears for an answer.

Lucky said, "Yes, I see. It seems we owe you an apology."

Bigman's gnomelike face screwed up unhappily. "But Lucky—"

Lucky shook his head. "Let go, Bigman! Never hang on to a theory after it's been exploded. I hope you understand, Mr. Norrich, that Bigman was only doing what he felt to be his duty."

"I wish he had asked a few questions before acting," said Norrich, coldly, "Now may I go? Do you mind?"

"You may go. As an official request, however, please make no mention of what has occurred to anyone. That's quite important."

Norrich said, "It comes under the heading of false arrest, I imagine, but we'll let it go. I won't mention this." He walked to the door, reached the signal patch with a minimum of fumbling, and walked out.

Bigman turned almost at once to Lucky. "It was a trick. You shouldn't have let him go."

Lucky rested his chin on the palm of his right hand, and his calm, brown eyes were thoughtful. "No, Bigman, he isn't the man we're after."

"But he's *got* to be, Lucky. Even if he's blind, *really* blind, it's an argument against him. Sure, Lucky," Bigman grew excited again, his small hands clumping into fists, "he could get close to the V-frog without seeing it. He could kill it."

Lucky shook his head. "No, Bigman. The V-frog's mental influence doesn't depend on its being seen. It's direct mental contact. That's the one fact we can't get around." He said slowly, "It had to be a robot who did that. It had to be, and Norrich is no robot."

"Well, how do you know he—?" But Bigman stopped.

"I see you've answered your own question. We sensed his emotion during our first meeting, when the V-frog was still with us. He has emotions, so he's not the robot and he's not the man we're looking for."

But even as he said so, there was a look of deep trouble on his face and he tossed the book-film on advanced robotics to one side as though despairing of help from it.

The first Agrav ship ever to be built was named *Jovian Moon* and it was not like any ship Lucky had ever seen. It was large enough to be a luxury liner of space, but the crew and passenger quarters were abnormally crowded forward, since nine tenths of the ship's volume consisted of the Agrav converter and the hyperatomic force-field condensers. From the midsection, curved vanes, ridged into a vague resemblance to bat's wings, extended on either side. Five to one side, five to the other, ten in all.

Lucky had been told that these vanes, in cutting the lines of force of the gravitational field, converted the gravity into hyperatomic energy. It was as prosaic as that, and yet they gave the ship an almost sinister appearance.

The ship rested now in a gigantic pit dug into Jupiter Nine. The lid, of reinforced concrete, had been retracted, and the whole area was under normal Jupiter Nine gravity and exposed to the normal airlessness of Jupiter Nine's surface.

Nevertheless the entire personnel of the project, nearly a thousand men, were gathered in this natural amphitheater. Lucky had never seen so many men in space suits at one time. There was a certain natural excitement because of the occasion; a certain almost hysterical restlessness that manifested itself in horseplay made possible by the low gravity.

Lucky thought grimly: And one of those men in space suits is no man at all.

But which one? And how could he tell?

Commander Donahue made his short speech of dedication to a group of men grown silent, impressed despite themselves; while Lucky, looking up at Jupiter, glanced at a small object near it that was not a star but a tiny sliver of light, curved like the paring of a small fingernail, almost too small for the curve to be seen. If there had been any air in the way, instead of Jupiter Nine's airless vacuum, that small curve would have been blurred into a formless spot of light.

Lucky knew the tiny crescent to be Ganymede, Jupiter Three, Jupiter's largest satellite and worthy moon of the giant planet. It was nearly three times the size of Earth's moon; it was larger than the planet Mercury. It was almost as large as Mars. With the Agrav fleet completed, Ganymede would quickly become a major world of the solar system.

Commander Donahue christened the ship at last in a voice husky with emotion, and then the assembled audience, in groups of five and six, entered the air-filled interior of the satellite through the various locks.

Only those who were to be aboard the *Jovian Moon* remained. One by one they climbed the ramp to the entrance lock, Commander Donahue first.

Lucky and Bigman were last to board. Commander Donahue turned away from the air lock as they entered, stiffly unfriendly.

Bigman leaned toward Lucky, to say tightly, "Did you notice, Lucky, that Red Summers is on board?"

"I know."

"He's the cobber who tried to kill you."

"I know, Bigman."

The ship was lifting now in what was at first a majestic creep. The surface gravity of Jupiter Nine was only one eightieth of Earth, and though the weight of the ship was still in the hundreds of tons, that was not the cause of the initial slowness. Even were gravity absent altogether, the ship would still retain its full content of matter and all the inertia that went with it. It would still be just as hard to put all that matter into motion, or, if it came to that, to stop it or change its direction of travel, once it had begun moving.

But first slowly, then more and more rapidly, the pit was left behind. Jupiter Nine shrank beneath them and became visible in the visiplates as a rugged gray rock. The constellations powdered the black sky and Jupiter was a bright marble.

James Panner approached them and placed an arm on the shoulder of each man. "Would you two gentlemen care to join me in my cabin for a meal? There'll be nothing to watch here in the viewing room for a while." His wide mouth pulled back in a grin that swelled the cords of his thick neck and made it seem no neck at all but a mere continuation of head.

"Thank you," Lucky said. "It's kind of you to invite us."

"Well," said Panner, "the commander isn't going to and the men are a little leery of you, too. I don't want you to get too lonely. It will be a long trip."

"Aren't you leery of me, Dr. Panner?" Lucky asked dryly.

"Of course not. You tested me, remember, and I passed."

Panner's cabin was a small one in which the three barely fitted. It was obvious that the quarters in this, the first Agrav ship, were as cramped as engineering ingenuity could make them. Panner broke out three cans of ship-ration, the concentrated food that was universally eaten on space ships. It was almost home to Lucky and Bigman; the smell of heating rations, the feeling of crowding walls, outside of which was the infinite emptiness of space, and, sounding through those walls, the steady vibrating hum of hyperatomic motors converting field energies into a directional thrust or, at the very least, powering the energy-consuming innards of the ship.

If ever the ancient belief of the "music of the spheres" could be said to have come literally true, it was in that hum of hyperatomics that was the very essential of space flight.

Panner said, "We're past Jupiter Nine's escape velocity now, which means we can coast without danger of falling back to its surface."

Lucky said, "That means we're in free fall down to Jupiter."

"With fifteen million miles to fall, yes. Once we've piled up enough velocity to make it worthwhile, we'll shift to Agrav."

He took a watch out of his pocket as he spoke. It was a large disc of gleaming, featureless metal. He pressed a small catch, and luminous figures appeared upon its face. A glowing line of white encircled it, turning red in a sweeping arc until the redness closed in upon itself and the arc turned white again.

Lucky said, "Are we scheduled to enter Agrav so soon?"

"Not very long," said Panner. He placed the watch on the table, and they ate silently.

Panner lifted the watch again. "A little under a minute. It should be completely automatic." Although the chief engineer spoke calmly enough, the hand that held the watch trembled very slightly.

Panner said, "Now," and there was silence. Complete silence.

The hum of the hyperatomics had stopped. The very power to keep the ship's lights on and its pseudo-grav field in operation were now coming from Jupiter's gravitational field.

Panner said, "On the nose! Perfect!" He put away his watch, and though the smile on his broad, homely face was a restrained one, it virtually shouted relief. "We're actually on an Agrav ship now in full Agrav operation."

Lucky was smiling, too. "Congratulations. I'm pleased to be on board."

"I imagine you are. You worked hard enough for it. Poor Donahue."

Lucky said gravely, "I'm sorry I had to push the commander so hard, but I had no choice. One way or another, I had to be on board."

Panner's eyes narrowed at the sudden gravity in Lucky's voice. "*Had* to be?"

"Had to be! It seems almost certain to me that on board this ship at the present moment is the spy we're looking for."

10

In the Vitals of the Ship

Panner stared blankly. Then, "Why?"

"The Sirians would certainly want to know how the ship actually worked. If their method of spying is fool-proof, as it has been till now, why not continue it on board the ship?"

"What you're saying, then, is that one of the fourteen men on board the *Jovian Moon* is a robot?"

"That is exactly what I mean."

"But the men aboard ship have been chosen long since."

"The Sirians would know the reasons for choosing and the method of choice just as they know everything else about the project and they would maneuver their humanoid robot so as to have him chosen."

"That's giving them a lot of credit," muttered Panner.

"I admit it," said Lucky. "There is an alternative."

"Which is?"

"That the humanoid robot is aboard as a stowaway."

"Very unlikely," said Panner.

"But quite possible. It might easily have boarded the

ship in the confusion before the commander made his christening speech. I tried to watch the ship then, but it was impossible. Furthermore, nine tenths of the ship seems to be made up of engine compartment, so there must be plenty of room to hide."

Panner thought about it. "Not as much room as you might think."

"Still we must search the ship. Will you do that, Dr. Panner?"

"I?"

"Certainly. As chief engineer, you would know the contents of the engine compartment better than anyone else. We'll go with you."

"Wait. It's a fool's errand."

"If there is no stowaway, Dr. Panner, we have still gained something. We'll know we can restrict our consideration to the men legally aboard ship."

"Just three of us?"

Lucky said quietly, "Whom can we trust to help us, when anyone we might ask might be the robot we're looking for? Let us not discuss this any further, Dr. Panner. Are you willing to help us search the ship? I am asking your help in my capacity as a member of the Council of Science."

Reluctantly Panner got to his feet. "I suppose I must then."

They clambered down the hand holds of the narrow shaft leading to the first engine level. The light was subdued and, naturally, indirect, so that the huge structures on either side cast no shadow.

There was no sound, no slightest hum to indicate activity or to show that vast forces were being trapped and dealt with. Bigman, looking about, was appalled to find that nothing seemed familiar; that of the ordinary workings of a space ship, such as that of their own *Shooting Starr*, nothing seemed left.

"Everything's closed in," he said.

Panner nodded and said in a low voice, "Everything is as automatic as possible. The need for human intervention has been cut to the minimum."

"What about repairs?"

"There shouldn't have to be any," the engineer said grimly. "We have alternate circuits and duplicated equipment at every step, all allowing for automatic cut-in after self-check."

Panner moved ahead, guiding them through the narrow openings but moving always slowly as though at any moment he expected someone, or some thing, to hurl itself murderously upon them.

Level by level, methodically moving out from the central shaft along the side channels, Panner probed each bit of room with the sureness of the expert.

Eventually they came to a halt at the very bottom, hard against the large tail jets through which the glowing hyperatomic forces (when the ship was in ordinary flight) pressed backward to push the ship forward.

From within the ship the test jets showed as four smooth pipes, each twice as thick as a man, burrowing into the ship and ending in the tremendous featureless structures that housed the hyperatomic motors.

Bigman said, "Hey, the jets! Inside!"

"No," said Panner.

"Why not? A robot could hide there fine. It's open space, but what's that to a robot?"

"Hyperatomic thrusts," said Lucky, "would be plenty

to it and there've been a number of those till an hour ago. No, the jets are out."

"Well, then," said Panner, "there's no one anywhere in the engine compartments. No thing, either."

"You're sure?"

"Yes. There isn't a place we haven't looked, and the route I followed made it impossible for anything to get around and behind us."

Their voices made small echoes in the lengths of shafts behind them.

Bigman said, "Sands of Mars, that leaves us with the fourteen regulars."

Lucky said thoughtfully, "Less than that. Three of the men aboard ship showed emotion: Commander Donahue, Harry Norrich, Red Summers. That leaves eleven."

Panner said, "Don't forget me. I disobeyed an order. That leaves ten."

"That raises an interesting point," said Lucky. "Do you know anything about robotics?"

"I?" said Panner. "Never dealt with a robot in my life."

"Exactly," said Lucky. "Earthmen invented the positronic robot and developed most of the refinements, yet, except for a few specialists, the Earth technician knows nothing about robotics, simply because we don't use robots to any extent. It isn't taught in the schools and it doesn't come up in practice. I myself know the Three Laws and not too much more. Commander Donahue couldn't even quote the Three Laws. The Sirians, on the other hand, with a robot-saturated economy, must be past masters at all the subtleties of robotics.

"Now I spent a good deal of time yesterday and to-day with a book-film on advanced robotics that I found in the project library. It was the only book on the subject, by the way."

"So?" said Panner.

"It became obvious to me that the Three Laws aren't as simple as one might think. . . . Let us move on, by the way. We can give the engine levels a double check on the way back." He was moving across this lowest level as he spoke, looking with keen interest at his surroundings.

Lucky continued, "For instance, I might think it would only be necessary to give each man on the ship a ridiculous order and note whether it be obeyed. As a matter of fact, I did think so. But that isn't necessarily true. It is theoretically possible to adjust the positronic brain of a robot to obey only those orders that belong naturally to the line of its duties. Orders that are contrary to those duties or irrelevant to them may still be obeyed provided that they are preceded by certain words which act as a code or by the person who gives the orders identifying himself in a certain way. In this manner a robot can be handled in all ways by its proper overseers and yet be insensitive to strangers."

Panner, who had placed his hands on the holds that would guide the men up to the next higher level, released them. He turned to face Lucky.

He said, "You mean when you told me to take off my shirt and I didn't obey, that meant nothing?"

"I say it could have meant nothing, Dr. Panner, since taking off your shirt at that moment was no part of your regular duties, and my order might not have been stated in the proper form."

"Then you're accusing me of being a robot?"

"No. It isn't likely that you are. The Sirians, in choosing some member of the project to replace by a robot, would scarcely choose the chief engineer. For the robot to do that job properly, it would have to know so much about Agrav that the Sirians couldn't supply the knowledge. Or, if they could, they would have no need to spy."

"Thanks," said Panner, sourly, turning toward the hand holds again, but now Bigman's voice rang out.

"Hold it, Panner!" The small Martian had his ready needle-gun in his fist. He said, "Wait a minute, Lucky, how do we know he knows anything about Agrav? We're just assuming that. He never showed us any knowledge. When the *Jovian Moon* shifted to Agrav, where was he? Sitting on his squatter in his quarters with us, that's where he was."

Lucky said, "I thought of that, too, Bigman, and that's one reason I brought Panner down here. He's obviously acquainted with the engines. I've watched him inspect everything and he couldn't have done it with such assurance if he weren't an expert on the workings."

"Does that suit you, Martian?" Panner demanded with suppressed anger.

Bigman put his needle-gun away, and without a further word Panner scrambled up the ladder.

They stopped off at the next level, working through it a second time.

Panner said, "All right, that leaves ten men: two army officers, four engineers, four workmen. What do you propose to do? X-ray each of them separately? Something like that?"

Lucky shook his head. "That's too risky. Apparently the Sirians have been known to use a cute little trick to protect themselves. They've been known to use robots to carry messages or to perform tasks which the individual giving the orders wanted to be kept secret. Now obviously a robot can't keep a secret if a human being asks him, in the proper fashion, to reveal it. What the Sirians do, then, is to install an explosive device in the robot which is triggered by any attempt to force the robot to give away the secret."

"You mean if you put an X-ray on the robot, it will explode?"

"There's a very good chance that it would. Its greatest secret is its identity, and it may be triggered for every attempt to discover that identity that the Sirians could think of." Lucky added regretfully, "They hadn't counted on a V-frog; there was no trigger against that. They had to order the robot to kill the V-frog directly. Or that might have been preferable anyway, since it managed to keep the robot alive undetected."

"Wouldn't the robot be harming humans nearby if it exploded? Wouldn't it be breaking First Law?" asked Panner with a trace of sarcasm.

"*It* wouldn't. It would have no control over the explosion. The triggering would be the result of the sound of a certain question or the sight of a certain action, not the result of anything the robot itself would do."

They crawled up to still another level.

"Then what do you expect to do, Councilman?" demanded Panner.

"I don't know," Lucky said frankly. "The robot must be made to give itself away somehow. The Three Laws, however modified and fancified, *must* apply. It's only a question of being sufficiently acquainted with robotics to know how to take advantage of those Laws. If I knew how to force the robot into some action that would show it to be non-human without activating any explosive device with which it might be equipped; if I could manipulate the Three Laws so as to force one to conflict with another sufficiently strongly to paralyze the creature completely; if I—"

Panner broke in impatiently, "Well, if you expect help from me, Councilman, it's no use. I've told you already I know nothing of robotics." He whirled suddenly. "What's that?"

Bigman looked about, too. "I didn't hear anything."

Wordlessly Panner squeezed past them, dwarfed by the bending metal tube on either side.

He had gone almost as far as he could, the other two following, when he muttered, "Someone might have squeezed in among the rectifiers. Let me pass again."

Lucky stared, frowning, into what was almost a forest of twisting cables that enclosed them in a complete dead end.

Lucky said, "It seems clear to me."

"We can test it for sure," Panner said tightly. He had opened a panel in the wall nearby and now he reached in cautiously, looking over his shoulder.

"Don't move," he said.

Bigman said testily, "Nothing's happened. There's nothing there."

Panner relaxed. "I know it. I asked you not to move because I didn't want to slice an arm off when I established the force field."

"What force field?"

"I've shorted a force field right across the corridor. You can't move out of there any more than you could if you were encased in solid steel three feet thick."

Bigman yelled, "Sands of Mars, Lucky, he *is* the robot!" His hand lunged.

Panner cried at once, "Don't try the needle-gun. Kill me and how do you ever get out?" He stared at them, dark eyes sparking, his broad shoulders hunched. "Remember, energy can get through a force field but matter can't, not even air molecules. You're airtight in there. Kill me and you'll suffocate long before anyone happens to come across you down here."

"I said he was the robot," said Bigman in raging despair.

Panner laughed shortly, "You're wrong. I'm not a robot. But if there *is* one, I know who it is."

11

Down the Line of Moons

"Who?" Bigman demanded at once.

But it was Lucky who answered. "Obviously he thinks it's one of us."

"Thanks!" said Panner. "How would *you* explain it? You mentioned stowaways; you talked about people forcing their way on board the *Jovian Moon*. Talk about nerve! Aren't there two people who did force their way on board? Didn't I witness the process? *You two!*"

"True enough," said Lucky.

"And you brought me down here so you could investigate every inch of the ship's workings. You tried to keep me busy with stories about robots hoping I wouldn't notice that you two were going over the whole ship with a microscope."

Bigman said, "We have a right to do it. This is Lucky Starr!"

"He *says* he's Lucky Starr. If he's a member of the Council of Science, he can prove it and he knows how. If I had any brains, I'd have demanded identification before taking you down."

"It's not too late now," Lucky said calmly. "Can you see clearly from that distance?" He held up one arm, palm forward, and peeled the sleeve back.

"I'm not coming any closer," Panner said angrily.

Lucky said nothing to that. He let his wrist tell the story. The skin along the inner surface of his wrist seemed merely exposed skin, but years before it had been treated hormonally in a most complicated fashion. Responding to nothing more than a disciplined effort of Lucky's will, an oval spot on the wrist darkened and slowly turned black. Within it, little yellow specks formed in the familiar patterns of the Big Dipper and of Orion.

Panner gasped as though the breath had been forcibly knocked out of his lungs. Few human beings had the occasion to see this sign of the Council, but all above the age of childhood knew it for what it was— the final and unforgeable identification insigne of the councilman of science.

Panner was left with no choice. Silently, reluctantly, he released the force field and stepped back.

Bigman came out, raging, "I ought to bend in your skull, you lopsided—"

Lucky pulled him back. "Forget it, Bigman. The man had as much right to suspect us as we had to suspect him. Settle down."

Panner shrugged. "It seemed logical."

"I admit it did. I think we can trust each other now."

"You, maybe," the chief engineer said pointedly. "You're identified. What about this little loudmouth with you? Who identifies him?"

Bigman squawked incoherently and Lucky stepped in between the two. "I identify him and take full responsibility for him. . . . Now I propose that we get back to passenger quarters before a search is organized for us. Everything that went on down here is, of course, strictly confidential."

Then, as though nothing had happened, they resumed the climb upward.

The room assigned to them contained a two-decker bed and a washstand out of which a small trickle of water could be urged. Nothing more. Even the cramped and Spartan quarters on board the *Shooting Starr* were luxury to this.

Bigman sat cross-legged on the upper bed, while Lucky sponged his neck and shoulders. They talked in whispers, conscious of the listening ears that might be present on the other side of the walls.

Bigman said, "Look, Lucky, suppose I go up to each person on board ship; I mean, each of the ten we don't know about? Suppose I deliberately pick a fight with each one, call them a few names, things like that? Wouldn't it turn out that the guy who doesn't take a punch at me is the robot?"

"Not at all. He might not want to break shipboard discipline, or he might know what a handy fellow you are with a needle-gun, or he might not want to get into a wrangle with the Council of Science, or he might just not like to hit a man smaller than himself."

"Aw, come on, Lucky." Bigman was silent for a minute, then he said cautiously, "I've been thinking: how can you be *sure* the robot is aboard ship? I keep thinking maybe it stayed back on Jupiter Nine. It's possible."

"I know it's possible and yet I'm sure the robot is here on board ship. That's just it. I'm sure and I don't know why I'm sure," said Lucky, his eyes dark with thought. He leaned against the bed and tapped his teeth with the knuckle of one finger. "That first day we landed on Jupiter Nine, something happened."

"What?"

"If I only knew! I had it; I knew what it was, or thought I did, just before I went to sleep that night, and it vanished. I haven't been able to get it back. If I were on Earth, I'd submit to a psycho-probe. Great Galaxy, I swear I would!

"I've tried every trick I could. Thinking hard, getting my mind off it altogether. When we were with Panner down in the engine levels, I tried talking my fool head off. I thought if I would just keep discussing every aspect of the matter, the thought was bound to pop into my head. It didn't.

"But it's there just the same. It's because of the thought that I must feel so sure the robot is one of the men aboard ship. I've made the subconscious deduction. If I could only put my finger on it, I'd have the whole answer. If I could only put my finger on it."

He sounded almost despairing.

Bigman had never seen Lucky with quite that look of frustrated loss in his face. He said, worried, "Hey, we'd better get some sleep."

"Yes, we'd better."

Minutes later, in the darkness, Bigman whispered, "Hey, Lucky, what makes you so sure I'm not the robot myself?"

Lucky whispered back, "Because the Sirians couldn't bear to build a robot with such an ugly face," and lifted his elbow to ward off a flying pillow.

The days passed. Halfway to Jupiter, they passed the inner and more sparsely populated belt of small

moons, of which only Six, Seven, and Ten were numbered. Jupiter Seven was visible as a bright star, but
the others were far enough away to melt into the
background of the constellations.

Jupiter itself had grown to the size of the moon
as seen from Earth. And because the ship was approaching the planet with the sun squarely to its rear,
Jupiter remained in the "full" phase. Its entire visible
surface was ablaze with sunlight. There was no shadow
of night advancing across it.

Yet though the size of the moon, it was not so bright
as the moon by any means. Its cloud-decked surface
reflected eight times as much of the light that reached
it, as did the bare powdered rock of the moon. The
trouble was that Jupiter only received one twenty-
seventh of the light per square mile that the moon did.
The result was that it was only one third as bright at
that moment as the moon appeared to be to human
beings on Earth.

Yet it was more spectacular than the moon. Its belts
had become quite distinct, brownish streaks with soft
fuzzy edges against a creamy-white background. It was
even easy to make out the flattened straw-colored
oval that was the Great Red Spot as it appeared at one
edge, crossed the face of the planet, then disappeared
at the other.

Bigman said, "Hey, Lucky, Jupiter looks as though
it isn't really round. Is that just an optical illusion?"

"Not at all," said Lucky. "Jupiter *really* isn't round.
It's flattened at the poles. You've heard that Earth is
flattened at the poles, haven't you?"

"Sure. But not enough to notice."

"Of course not. Consider! Earth is twenty-five thousand miles about its equator and rotates in twenty-four

hours, so that a spot on its equator moves just over a thousand miles an hour. The resulting centrifugal force bulges the equator outward so that the diameter of the Earth across its middle is about twenty-seven miles more than the diameter from North Pole to South Pole. The difference in the two diameters is only about a third of one per cent so that from space Earth looks like a perfect sphere."

"Oh."

"Now take Jupiter. It is 276,000 miles about its equator, eleven times the circumference of Earth, yet it rotates about its axis in only ten hours; five minutes less than that, to be exact. A point on its equator is moving at a speed of almost twenty-eight thousand miles an hour; or twenty-eight times as fast as any point on Earth. There's a great deal more centrifugal force and a much larger equatorial bulge, especially since the material in Jupiter's outer layers is much lighter than that in the Earth's crust. Jupiter's diameter across its equator is nearly six thousand miles more than its diameter from North Pole to South Pole. The difference in the diameters is a full fifteen per cent, and that's an easy thing to see."

Bigman stared at the flattened circle of light that was Jupiter and muttered, "Sands of Mars!"

The sun remained behind them and unseen as they sank toward Jupiter. They crossed the orbit of Callisto, Jupiter Four, outermost of Jupiter's major satellites, but did not see it to advantage. It was a world one and a half million miles from Jupiter and as large as Mercury, but it was on the other side of its orbit, a small pea close to Jupiter and heading into eclipse in its shadow.

Ganymede, which was Jupiter Three, was close enough to show a disc one third as wide as the moon seen from Earth. It lay off to one side so that part of its night surface could be seen. It was three quarters full even so, pale white, and featureless.

Lucky and Bigman found themselves ignored by the rest of the crew. The commander never spoke to them or even looked at them, but moved past with eyes fixed on nothingness. Norrich, when he was led past by Mutt, nodded cheerfully as he always did when he detected the presence of humans. When Bigman answered the greeting, however, the pleasant look vanished from his face. A gentle pressure on Mutt's harness started the dog moving and he was gone.

The two found it more comfortable to eat in their own quarters.

Bigman grumbled. "Who in space do they think they are? Even that guy Panner gets busy all at once when I'm around."

Lucky said, "In the first place, Bigman, when the commander makes it so obvious that we're in his bad books, subordinates don't fall over themselves being friendly. Secondly, our dealings with a few of the men have been unpleasant."

Bigman said thoughtfully, "I met Red Summers today, the cobber. There he was coming out of the engine room and there I was, facing him."

"What happened? You didn't . . ."

"I didn't do anything. I just stood there waiting for him to start something, *hoping* he would start something, but he just smiled and moved around me."

Everyone aboard the *Jovian Moon* was watching the day Ganymede eclipsed Jupiter. It wasn't a true eclipse.

Ganymede covered only a tiny part of Jupiter. Ganymede was 600,000 miles away, not quite half the size of the moon as seen from Earth. Jupiter was twice the distance, but it was a swollen globe now, fourteen times as wide as Ganymede, menacing and frightening.

Ganymede met Jupiter a little below the latter's equator, and slowly the two globes seemed to melt together. Where Ganymede cut in, it made a circle of dimmer light, for Ganymede had far less of an atmosphere than Jupiter had and reflected a considerably smaller portion of the light it received. Even if that had not been so, it would have been visible as it cut across Jupiter's belts.

The remarkable part was the crescent of blackness that hugged Ganymede's rear as the satellite moved completely onto Jupiter's disk. As the men explained to one another in breathless whispers, it was Ganymede's shadow falling on Jupiter.

The shadow, only its edge seen, moved with Ganymede, but slowly gained on it. The sliver of black cut finer and finer until in the mid-eclipse region, when Jupiter, Ganymede, and the *Jovian Moon* all made a straight line with the sun, the shadow was completely gone, covered by the world that cast it.

Thereafter, as Ganymede continued to move on, the shadow began to advance, appearing before it, first a sliver, then a thicker crescent, until both left Jupiter's globe.

The entire eclipse lasted three hours.

The *Jovian Moon* reached and passed the orbit of Ganymede when that satellite was at the other end of its seven-day orbit about Jupiter.

There was a special celebration when that happened. Men with ordinary ships (not often, to be sure) had reached Ganymede and landed on it, but no one, not one human being, had ever penetrated closer than that to Jupiter. And now the *Jovian Moon* did.

The ship passed within one hundred thousand miles of Europa, Jupiter Two. It was the smallest of Jupiter's major satellites, only nineteen hundred miles in diameter. It was slightly smaller than the moon, but its closeness made it appear twice the size of the moon as seen from Earth. Dark markings could be made out that might have been mountain ranges. Ship's telescopes proved they were exactly that. The mountains resembled those on Mercury, and there was no sign of moon-like craters. There were brilliant patches, too, resembling ice fields.

And still they sank downward, and left Europa's orbit behind.

Io was the innermost of Jupiter's major satellites, in size almost exactly equal to Earth's moon. Its distance from Jupiter, moreover, was only 285,000 miles, or little more than that of the moon from Earth.

But there the kinship ended. Whereas Earth's gentle gravitational field moved the moon about itself in the space of four weeks, Io, caught in Jupiter's gravity, whipped about in its slightly larger orbit in the space of forty-two hours. Where the moon moved about Earth at a speed of a trifle over a thousand miles an hour, Io moved about Jupiter at a speed of twenty-two thousand miles an hour, and a landing upon it was that much more difficult.

The ship, however, maneuvered perfectly. It cut in ahead of Io and wiped out Agrav at just the proper moment.

With a bound, the hum of the hyperatomics was back, filling the ship with what seemed a cascade of sound after the silence of the past weeks.

The *Jovian Moon* curved out of its path, finally, subject once again to the accelerating effect of a gravitational field, that of Io. It was established in an orbit about the satellite at a distance of less than ten thousand miles, so that Io's globe filled the sky.

They circled about it from dayside to nightside, coming lower and lower. The ship's batlike Agrav fins were retracted in order that they might not be torn off by Io's thin atmosphere.

Then, eventually, there was the keen whistling that came with the friction of ship against the outermost wisps of that atmosphere.

Velocity dropped and dropped; so did altitude. The ship's sidejets curved it to face stern-downward toward Io, and the hyperatomic jets sprang into life, cushioning the fall. Finally, with one last bit of drop and the softest jar, the *Jovian Moon* came to rest on the surface of Io.

There was wild hysteria on board the *Jovian Moon*. Even Lucky and Bigman had their backs pounded by men who had been avoiding them constantly all voyage long.

One hour later, in the darkness of Io's night, with Commander Donahue in the lead, the men of the *Jovian Moon,* each in his space suit, emerged one by one onto the surface of Jupiter One.

Sixteen men. The first human beings ever to land on Io!

Correction, thought Lucky. Fifteen men.

And one robot!

12

The Skies and Snows of Io

It was Jupiter they stopped to look at. It was Jupiter that held them frozen. There was no talk about it, no babble over the helmet radios. It was beyond talk.

Jupiter was a giant globe which, from rim to rim, extended one eighth of the way across the visible sky. Had it been full, it would have been two thousand times as bright as the Earth's full moon, but the night shadow cut a third of it away.

The bright zones and dark belts that crossed it were not merely brown now. They were close enough to show full clear color: pink, green, blue, and purple, amazingly bright. The edges of the bands were ragged and slowly changed shape as they watched, as though the atmosphere were being whipped into gigantic and turbulent storms, as most probably it was. Io's clear, thin atmosphere didn't obscure the smallest detail of that colored shifting surface.

The Great Red Spot was heaving ponderously into sight. It gave the impression of a funnel of gas, swirling lazily.

They watched for a long time, and Jupiter did not

change position. The stars moved past it, but Jupiter remained fixed where it was, low in the western sky. It could not move, since Io presented only one side to Jupiter as it revolved. On nearly half of Io's surface Jupiter never rose, and on nearly half it never set. In an in-between region of the satellite, a region making up nearly a fifth of the total surface, Jupiter remained forever on the horizon, part showing, part hidden.

"What a place for a telescope!" murmured Bigman on the wave length allotted to Lucky during the pre-landing briefing.

Lucky said, "They'll have one soon and a lot of other equipment."

Bigman touched Lucky's face-plate to attract his attention and pointed quickly. "Look at Norrich. Poor guy, he can't see any of this!"

Lucky said, "I noticed him before. He's got Mutt with him."

"Yes. Sands of Mars, they go to trouble for that Norrich! That dog suit is a special job. I was watching them put it on the dog when you were keeping tabs on the landing. They had to test to make sure he could hear the orders and obey them and if he'd let Norrich use him once Norrich got into a space suit. Apparently it all worked out."

Lucky nodded. On impulse he moved rapidly in Norrich's direction. Io's gravity was just a trifle over that of the moon, and both he and Bigman could handle that neatly.

A few long, flat strides did the job. "Norrich," said Lucky, shifting to the engineer's wave length.

One cannot tell direction of a sound when it comes

out of earphones, of course, and Norrich's blind eyes looked about helplessly. "Who is it?"

"Lucky Starr." He was facing the blind man, and through the face-plate could make out clearly the look of intense joy on Norrich's face. "You're happy to be here?"

"Happy? You might call it that. Is Jupiter very beautiful?"

"Very. Would you want me to describe it to you?"

"No. You don't have to. I've seen it by telescope when—when I had eyes, and I can see it in my mind now. It's just that . . . I don't know if I can make you understand. We're some of the few people to stand on a new world for the first time. Do you realize what a special group that makes us?"

His hand reached down to stroke Mutt's head and contacted only the metal of the dog's helmet, of course. Through the curved face-plate, Lucky could see the dog's lolling tongue, and his uneasy eyes turning restlessly this way and that, as though disturbed by the strange surroundings or by the presence of his master's voice without the familiar body that went with it.

Norrich said quietly, "Poor Mutt! The low gravity has him all confused. I won't keep him out much longer."

Then, with an increase of passion again, "Think of all the trillions of people in the galaxy. Think how few of them have had the luck to be the first on a world. You can almost name them all off. Janofski and Sterling were the first men on the moon, Ching the first man on Mars, Lubell and Smith on Venus. Add them all up. Even count in all the asteroids and all the planets outside the solar system. Add up all the firsts and see how few there are. And we're among those few. *I*'m among those few."

He flung his arms out as though he were ready to embrace the whole satellite. "And I owe that to Summers, too. When he worked out a new technique for manufacturing the lead contact point—it was just a matter of a bent rotor, but it saved two million dollars and a year's time, and he not even a trained mechanic—they offered to let him be in the party as reward. You know what he said. He said I deserved it in his place. They said sure, but I was blind, and he reminded them why I was blind and said he wouldn't go without me. So they took us both. I know you two don't think much of Summers, but that's what I think of when *I* think of him."

The commander's voice sounded ringingly in all helmets: "Let's get to work, men. Jupiter will stay where it is. Look at it later."

For hours the ship was unloaded, equipment was set up, tents unfurled. Temporary air tights were prepared for possible use as oxygen-supplied headquarters outside the ship.

The men were not to be kept from watching the unusual sky, though. As it happened, all three of Jupiter's other large satellites were in the sky.

Europa was closest, appearing somewhat smaller than Earth's moon. It was a crescent, near the eastern horizon. Ganymede, appearing smaller still, was nearer zenith and half full. Callisto, only a quarter the width of Earth's moon, was nudging close to Jupiter and, like Jupiter, was some two thirds full. All three together gave not one quarter the light of Earth's full moon and were completely inconspicuous in the presence of Jupiter.

Bigman said exactly that.

Lucky looked down at his small Martian friend after having studied the eastern horizon thoughtfully. "You think nothing could beat Jupiter, do you?"

"Not out here," Bigman said stoutly.

"Then keep watching," said Lucky.

In Io's thin atmosphere there was no twilight to speak of and no warning. There was a diamondlike sparkle along the frost-covered top-line of the ridge of low hills, and seven seconds later the sun had topped the horizon.

It was a tiny seed-pearl of a sun, a little circle of brilliant white, and for all the light that giant Jupiter cast, the pigmy sun cast much, much more.

They got the telescope up in time to catch Callisto vanishing behind Jupiter. One by one, all three satellites would do the same. Io, although it kept only one face to Jupiter, revolved about it in forty-two hours. That meant that the sun and all the stars seemed to march around Io's skies in those forty-two hours.

As for the satellites, Io moved faster than any of them, so it kept overtaking them in the race about Jupiter. It overtook the farthest and slowest, Callisto, most rapidly; so Callisto circled Io's heavens in two days. Ganymede took four days and Europa seven. Each traveled from east to west and each in due turn was to pass behind Jupiter.

The excitement in the case of the Callisto eclipse, which was the first to be witnessed, was extreme. Even Mutt seemed to be affected by it. He had grown increasingly used to low gravity, and Norrich gave him periods of freedom during which he floundered grotesquely about and tried vainly to inspect by nose the numerous strange things he encountered. And in the end, when Callisto reached Jupiter's glowing curve and passed behind, and all the men grew silent, Mutt, too, sat on his swathed haunches and, tongue lolling, stared upward at the sky.

But it was the sun they were really waiting for. Its apparent motion was faster than that of any of the satellites. It gained on Europa (whose crescent thinned to nothingness) and passed behind it, remaining in eclipse for something less than thirty seconds. It emerged, and then Europa was a crescent again, with its horns facing in the other direction now.

Ganymede had plunged behind Jupiter before the sun could reach it, and Callisto, having emerged from behind Jupiter, was below the horizon.

It was the sun and Jupiter now, those two.

The men watched greedily as the seed-pearl sun climbed higher in the sky. As it did, Jupiter's phase grew narrower, its lighted portion always, of course, facing the sun. Jupiter became a "half-moon," then a fat crescent, then a thin one.

In Io's thin atmosphere the sunlit sky was a deep purple, and only the dimmer stars had been blotted out. Against that background there burnt the gigantic crescent in the sky, bulging out toward the relentlessly approaching sun.

It was like David's pebble hurled from some cosmic slingshot toward Goliath's forehead.

The light of Jupiter shrank still further and became a yellowish curved thread. The sun was almost touching.

It did touch and the men cheered. They had masked their face-plates in order to watch, but now that was no longer necessary, for the light had dimmed to bearable dimensions.

Yet it had not vanished entirely. The sun had moved behind the edge of Jupiter but it still shone murkily through that giant planet's thick, deep atmosphere of hydrogen and helium.

Jupiter itself was now completely blanked out, but its atmosphere had sprung to life, refracting and bending the sunlight through itself and around the curve of the planet, a smoothly bending film of milky light.

The film of light spread as the sun moved farther behind Jupiter. It curved back on itself until faintly, very faintly, the two horns of light met on Jupiter's other side. Jupiter's vanished body was outlined in light and one side bulged with it. It was a diamond ring in the sky, big enough to hold two thousand globes the size of the moon as seen from Earth.

And still the sun moved farther behind Jupiter so that the light began to fade and grow dim, and dimmer, until finally it was gone and, except for the pale crescent of Europa, the sky was black and belonged to the stars.

"It will stay like this five hours," said Lucky to Bigman. "Then everything will repeat itself in reverse as the sun comes out."

"And this happens every forty-two hours?" said Bigman, awed.

"That's right," said Lucky.

Panner approached them the next day and called out to them, "How are you? We're almost done here." He spread his arm about in a broad circle to indicate the Ioan valley, now littered with equipment. "We'll be leaving soon, you know, and we'll leave most of this stuff here."

"We will?" said Bigman, surprised.

"Why not? There's nothing living on the satellite to disturb the stuff and there's no weather to speak of. Everything's coated for protection against the ammonia in the atmosphere and it will keep nicely till a second expedition comes round." His voice was suddenly lower. "Is there anyone else on your private wave length, Councilman?"

"My receivers don't detect anyone."

"Do you want to take a walk with me?" He headed out, out of the shallow valley and up the gentle slope of the surrounding hills. The other two followed.

Panner said, "I must ask your pardon if I seemed unfriendly on board ship. I thought it better so."

"There are no hard feelings," Lucky assured him.

"I thought I'd try an investigation of my own, you see, and I thought it safer not to seem hand in glove with you. I was sure that if I only watched carefully, I would catch someone giving himself away, doing something non-human, if you know what I mean. I failed, I'm afraid."

They had reached the top of the first rise and Panner

looked back. He said with amusement, "Look at that dog, will you? He's getting the real feel of low gravity."

Mutt had learned a lot in the past few days. His body arched and straightened as he lunged in low, twenty-foot leaps, and he seemed to indulge in them for the sheerest pleasure.

Panner switched his radio to the wave length that had been reserved for Norrich's use in calling Mutt and shouted, "Hey, Mutt, hey, boy, come, Mutt," and whistled.

The dog heard, of course, and bounded high in the air. Lucky switched to the dog's wave length and heard his delighted barking.

Panner waved his arm and the dog headed toward them, then stopped and looked back as though wondering if he did right to leave his master. He approached more slowly.

The men walked onward again. Lucky said, "A Sirian robot built to fool a man would be a thorough job. Casual examination wouldn't detect the fraud."

"Mine wasn't casual examination," protested Panner.

Lucky's voice held more than a tinge of bitterness. "I'm beginning to think that the examination by anyone but an experienced robotics man can be nothing *but* casual."

They were passing over a drift of snowlike material, glittering in Jupiter light, and Bigman looked down upon it in amazement.

"This thing melts if you look at it," he said. He picked some up in his gauntleted hand, and it melted down and ran off like butter on a stove. He looked back, and where the three had stepped were deep indentations.

Lucky said, "It's not snow, it's frozen ammonia, Bigman. Ammonia melts at a temperature eighty degrees lower than ice does, and the heat radiating from our suits melts it that much faster."

Bigman lunged forward to where the drifts lay deeper, gouging holes wherever he stepped, and shouted, "This is fun."

Lucky called, "Make sure your heater is on if you're going to play in the snow."

"It's on," yelled Bigman, and running down a ridge with long low leaps, he flung himself headlong into a bank. He moved like a diver in slow motion, hit the drifted ammonia, and, for a moment, disappeared. He floundered to his feet.

"It's like diving into a cloud, Lucky. You hear me? Come on, try it. More fun than sand skiing on the moon."

"Later, Bigman," Lucky said. Then he turned to Panner. "For instance, did you try in any way to test any of the men?"

Out of the corner of his eye Lucky could see Bigman plunging into a bank for a second time, and, after a few moments had elapsed, his eyes turned full in that direction. Another moment and he called out anxiously, "Bigman!" Then, more loudly and much more anxiously, "*Bigman!*"

He started running.

Bigman's voice came, weak and gasping. "Breath ... knocked out . . . hit rock . . . river down here . . ."

"Hold on, I'll be with you." Lucky and Panner, too, were devouring space with their strides.

Lucky knew what had happened, of course. The surface temperature of Io was not far removed from the melting point of ammonia. Underneath the ammonia drifts, melting ammonia could be feeding hidden rivers of that foul-smelling, choking substance that existed so copiously on the outer planets and their satellites.

There was the rattle of Bigman's coughing in his ear. "Break in air hose . . . ammonia getting in . . . choking."

Lucky reached the hole left by Bigman's diving body and looked down. The ammonia river was plainly visible, bubbling slowly downhill over sharp crags. It must have been against one of those that Bigman's air hose had been damaged.

"Where are you, Bigman?"

And though Bigman answered feebly, "Here," he was nowhere to be seen.

13

Fall!

Lucky jumped recklessly into the exposed river, drifting gently downward under the pull of Io's weak gravity. He was angry at the slowness of his fall, at Bigman for the childish enthusiasms that seized him so suddenly, and—unpredictably—at himself for not having stopped Bigman when he might.

Lucky hit the stream, and ammonia sprayed high in the air, then fell back with surprising quickness. Io's thin atmosphere could not support the small droplets even at low gravity.

There was no sense of buoyancy to the ammonia river. Lucky had not expected any to speak of. Liquid ammonia was less dense than water and had less lifting power. Nor was the force of the current great under Io's weak pull. Had Bigman not damaged his air hose, it would have been only a matter of walking out of the river and through any of the drifts that might have packed it round.

As it was . . .

Lucky splashed downstream furiously. Somewhere ahead the small Martian must be struggling feebly against the poisonous ammonia. If the break in the hose was large enough, or had grown large enough, to allow liquid ammonia to enter, Lucky would be too late.

He might be too late, already, and his chest constricted and tightened at the thought.

A form streaked past Lucky, burying itself in the powdered ammonia. It disappeared, leaving a tunnel into which ammonia slowly collapsed.

"Panner," Lucky said tentatively.

"Here I am." The engineer's arm fell upon Lucky's shoulder from behind. "That was Mutt. He came running when you yelled. We were both on his wave length."

Together they forged through the ammonia on the track of the dog. They met him, returning.

Lucky cried eagerly, "He's got Bigman."

Bigman's arms feebly enfolded the dog's suit-encased haunches, and though that hampered Mutt's movements, low gravity enabled the dog to make respectable headway through use of shoulder muscles alone.

Even as Lucky bent for Bigman, the little Martian's straining hold relaxed and he fell.

Lucky scooped him up. He wasted no time on investigation or talk. There was only one thing to do. He turned up Bigman's oxygen flow to full capacity, slung him over his shoulders, and ran for the ship. Even allowing for Io's gravity he had never run so recklessly in his life. With such haste did he kick the ground away when coming down from each hurtling, horizontal stride that the effect was almost one of low-level flying.

Panner pumped along in the rear, and Mutt stayed excitedly at Lucky's heels.

Lucky used the communal wave length to alert the others even as he was running and one of the air tights was made ready.

Lucky hurtled inside the air tight, scarcely breaking his stride. The flap closed behind him and the interior flooded with additional air under pressure to make up the loss during the flap's opening.

With flying fingers he unbuckled Bigman's helmet, then more slowly drew off the rest of the suit.

He felt for the heartbeat and, to his relief, found it. The air tight was equipped, of course, with a first-aid kit. He made the necessary injections for general stimulation and waited for warmth and plentiful oxygen to do the rest.

And eventually Bigman's eyes fluttered and focused with difficulty on Lucky. His lips moved and made the word "Lucky," though no sound was involved.

Lucky laughed with relief and finally took the time to remove his own space suit.

On board the *Jovian Moon* Harry Norrich stopped at the open door of the compartment within which Bigman was completing his recuperation. His unseeing, china-blue eyes were warm with pleasure.

"How's the invalid?"

Bigman struggled up in his bunk and shouted, "Fine! Sands of Mars, I feel great! If it weren't that Lucky wants to keep me down, I'd be up and around."

Lucky grunted his disbelief.

Bigman ignored that. He said, "Hey, let Mutt come in. Good old Mutt! Here, boy, here!"

Mutt, the hold on his harness released, trotted over

to Bigman, his tail wagging furiously and his intelligent eyes doing everything but talk a greeting.

Bigman's small arm embraced the dog's neck in a bear hug. "Boy, *there's* a friend. You heard what he did, Norrich, didn't you?"

"Everyone did," and it was plain to see that Norrich took a great personal pride in his dog's accomplishment.

"I just barely remember it," Bigman said, "before I blacked out altogether. I got that lungful of ammonia and couldn't seem to straighten out. I rolled downhill, just going through the ammonia snow as though it were nothing. Then there was this thing coming at me and I was sure it was Lucky when I heard the sound of something moving. But he knocked enough of the snow off us to let some of the Jupiter light come in and I could just make out it was Mutt. The last thing I remember was grabbing him."

"And a good thing, too," Lucky said. "The extra time that would have been required for me to find you would have been your finish."

Bigman shrugged. "Aw, Lucky, you make such a big deal out of it. Nothing would have happened if I hadn't just caught the hose on a rock and torn it. At that if I had had enough brains to turn up my oxygen pressure, I could have kept the ammonia out. It was just the first lungful that seemed to put me out of kilter. I couldn't think."

Panner passed by, just then, and looked. "How are you, Bigman?"

"Sands of Mars! Looks like everyone thinks I'm an invalid or something. There's nothing wrong with me.

Even the commander stopped by and managed to find his tongue long enough to grunt at me."

"Well," said Panner, "maybe he's getting over his mad."

"Never," said Bigman. "He just wants to make sure his first flight won't be spoiled by a casualty. He wants his record pure white, that's all."

Panner laughed. "All set for the take-off?"

Lucky said, "Are we leaving Io?"

"Any hour. The men are reloading the equipment we're taking with us and securing what we leave behind. If you two can make the pilot room once we're underway, do so. We'll get a better look at Jupiter than ever."

He tickled Mutt behind one ear and left

They radioed Jupiter Nine that they were leaving Io, as days earlier they had radioed that they had surfaced on the satellite.

Bigman said, "Why don't we call Earth? Chief Councilman Conway ought to know we've made it."

"Officially," said Lucky, "we haven't made it all the way until we've returned to Jupiter Nine."

He did not add aloud that he was not at all anxious to return to Jupiter Nine, still less anxious to talk to Conway. He had, after all, accomplished nothing on this trip.

His brown eyes surveyed the control room. The engineers and crewmen were at their stations for the takeoff. The commander, his two officers and Panner, however, were in the control room.

Lucky wondered again about the officers as time and again he had wondered about each of the ten men whom the V-frog had not had a chance to eliminate.

He had spoken to each of them on occasion, as had Panner even more frequently. He had searched their quarters. He and Panner together had gone over their records. Nothing had resulted.

He would be going back to Jupiter Nine with the robot unlocated, and thereafter location would be harder than ever and he might have to report back to Council headquarters with news of failure.

Once more, desperately, the thought of X rays entered his mind, or some other means of forceful inspection. As always, he thought at once of the possibility of triggering off an explosion, probably a nuclear explosion.

It would destroy the robot. It would also kill thirteen men and blow up a priceless ship. Worst of all, it would show no safe way of detecting the humanoid robots which, Lucky felt certain, were preying in other parts of the Solar Confederation.

He was startled by Panner's sudden cry, "Here we go!"

There was the familiar distant *whoosh* of the initial thrust, the gathering backward press of acceleration, and Io's surface dropped away, faster and faster.

The visiplate could not center Jupiter in its entirety: it was too large. It centered the Great Red Spot instead and followed it in its rotation about the globe.

Panner said, "We've gone into Agrav again, yes, but it's only temporary, just to let Io pull away from us."

"But we're still falling toward Jupiter," Bigman said.

"That's right, but only till the proper moment is reached. Then we go into hyperatomic drive and plunge toward Jupiter on a hyperbolic orbit. Once that is established, we cut the drive and let Jupiter do the work. Our closest approach will be about 150,000 miles. Jupiter's gravity will zoom us around as though we were a pebble in a slingshot and shoot us out again. At the proper point our hyperatomic drive cuts in again. By taking advantage of the slingshot effect, we actually save a bit on energy over the alternative of leaving directly from Io, *and* we get some super close-ups of Jupiter."

He looked at his watch. "Five minutes," he said.

He was referring, as Lucky knew, to the moment when the ship would switch from Agrav to hyper-atomic drive and begin to curve off into the planned orbit about Jupiter.

Still staring at his watch, Panner said, "The time is selected so that we come out heading toward Jupiter Nine as squarely as possible. The fewer side adjustments we have to make, the more energy we save. We've got to come back to Jupiter Nine with as much of our original energy store as possible. The more we come back with, the better Agrav looks. I've set my goals at eighty-five per cent. If we can come back with ninety, that would be superlative."

Bigman said, "Suppose you come back with more energy than you had when you left? How would that be?"

"Super-superlative, Bigman, but impossible. There's something called the second law of thermodynamics that stands in the way of making a profit on the deal or, for that matter, of breaking even. We've got to take some loss." He smiled broadly and said, "One minute."

And at the appropriate second the sound of the

hyperatomics filled the ship with its muted murmurings, and Panner placed his watch in his pocket with a satisfied expression.

"From here on in," he said, "until actual landing maneuvers at the Jupiter Nine approach, everything is quite automatic."

He had no sooner said that when the humming ceased again, the lights in the room flickered and went out. Almost at once they went on again, but now there was a little red sign on the control panel that said, EMERGENCY.

Panner sprang to his feet. "What in Space . . .?"

He left the pilot room at a run, leaving the others staring after him and at one another in various degrees of horror. The commander had gone dead-white, his lined face a tired mask.

Lucky, with sudden decision, followed Panner, and Bigman, of course, followed Lucky.

They came upon one of the engineers clambering out of the engine compartment. He was panting. "Sir!"

"What is it, man?" snapped Panner.

"The Agrav is off, sir. It can't be activated."

"What about the hyperatomics?"

"The main reserve is shorted. We cut it just in time to keep it from blowing. If we touch it, the whole ship will go up. Every bit of the stored energy will blow."

"Then we're working on the emergency reservoir?"

"That's right."

Panner's swarthy face was congested with blood. "What good is that? We can't set up an orbit about Jupiter with the emergency reservoir. Out of the way. Let me down there."

The engineer stepped aside, and Panner swung into the shaft. Lucky and Bigman were at his heels.

Lucky and Bigman had not been in the engine compartment since that first day aboard the *Jovian Moon*. The scene was different now. There was no august silence, no sensation of mighty forces quietly at work.

Instead, the puny sound of men rose high about them.

Panner sprang off into the third level. "Now what's wrong?" he called. "Exactly what's wrong?"

Men parted to let him through and they all huddled over the gutted insides of a complex mechanism, pointing things out in tones of mingled despair and anger.

There were sounds of other footsteps coming down the rungs of the shaft, and then the Commander himself made his appearance.

He spoke to Lucky, who was standing gravely to one side. "What is it, Councilman?" It was the first time he had addressed Lucky since they had left Jupiter Nine.

Lucky said, "Serious damage of some sort, Commander."

"How did it happen? *Panner!*"

Panner looked up from the close examination of something that had been held out to him. He shouted in annoyance, "What in space do you want?"

Commander Donahue's nostrils flared. "Why has something been allowed to go wrong?"

"Nothing has been *allowed* to go wrong."

"Then what do you call this?"

"Sabotage, Commander. Deliberate, murdering sabotage!"

"*What!*"

"Five gravitic relays have been completely smashed and the necessary replacements have been removed and can't be located. The hyperatomic thrust-control has been fused and shorted beyond repair. None of it happened by accident."

The commander stared at his chief engineer. He said, hollowly, "Can anything be done?"

"Maybe the five relay replacements can be located or cannibalized out of the rest of the ship. I'm not sure. Maybe a makeshift thrust-control can be set up. It would take days anyway and I couldn't guarantee results."

"Days!" cried the commander. "It can't take days. *We're falling toward Jupiter!*"

There was a complete silence for a few moments, and then Panner put into words what all of them knew. "That's right, Commander. We're falling toward Jupiter and we can't stop ourselves in time. It means we're through, Commander. We're all dead men!"

14

Jupiter Close Up

It was Lucky who broke the deadly silence that followed, in sharp, incisive tones. "No man is dead while he has a mind capable of thought. Who can handle this ship's computer most rapidly?"

Commander Donahue said, "Major Brant. He's the regular trajectory man."

"Is he up in the control room?"

"Yes."

"Let's get to him. I want the detailed *Planetary Ephemerae* . . . Panner, you stay here with the men and get to work cannibalizing and improvising."

"What good will it—?" Panner began.

Lucky cut in at once. "Perhaps no good at all. If so, we'll hit Jupiter and you'll die after having wasted a few hours of labor. Now I've given you an order. Get to work!"

"But . . ." Commander Donahue seemed stuck after that one word.

Lucky said, "As councilman of science, I'm assuming command of this vessel. If you wish to dispute that, I'll have Bigman lock you in your cabin and you

can argue it out at the court-martial proceedings, assuming we survive."

Lucky turned away and moved quickly up the central shaft. Bigman motioned Commander Donahue
up with a quick jerk of his thumb and followed last.

Panner looked after them scowling, turned savagely
to the engineers, and said, "All right, you bunch of
corpses. No use waiting for it with our fingers in
our mouths. Hop to it."

Lucky strode into the control room.

The officer at the controls said, "What's wrong
down there?" His lips were white.

"You're Major Brant," said Lucky, "We haven't
been formally introduced, but never mind that. I'm
Councilman David Starr, and you're taking orders
from me. Get at that computer and do what you're
told with all the speed you have."

Lucky had the *Planetary Ephemerae* before him.
Like all great reference works, it was in book form
rather than film. The turning of pages, after all, made
for the more rapid location of a specific piece of information, than did the long-drawn-out unwinding of
film from end to end.

He turned the pages now with practiced hand,
searching among the rows and columns of numbers
that located the position of every chunk of matter in
the solar system over ten miles in diameter (and some
under) at certain standard times, together with their
planes of revolution and velocity of motion.

Lucky said, "Take the following co-ordinates as I
call them out, together with the line of motion, and
calculate the characteristics of the orbit and the posi-

tion of the point at this moment and for succeeding moments for the space of forty-eight hours."

The major's fingers flew as figures were converted by the special punch machine into a coded tape which was fed into the computer.

Even while that was taking place, Lucky said, "Calculate from our present position and velocity our orbit with respect to Jupiter and the point of intersection with the object whose orbit you have just calculated."

Again the major worked.

The computer spat out its results in coded tape that wound on to a spool and dictated the tapping of a typewriter that spelled out the results in figures.

Lucky said, "At the point of intersection, what is time discrepancy between our ship and the object?"

Again the major worked. He said, "We miss it by four hours, twenty-one minutes, and forty-four seconds."

"Calculate how the velocity of the ship must be altered in order to hit the point squarely. Use one hour from now as the starting time."

Commander Donahue broke in. "We can't do anything this close to Jupiter, Councilman. The emergency power won't break us away. Don't you understand that?"

"I'm not asking the major to break us away, Commander. I'm asking him to accelerate the ship toward Jupiter, for whatever our reserve power is worth."

The commander rocked back on his heels. *"Toward* Jupiter?"

The computer was making the calculation and the results were coming in. Lucky said, "Can you accelerate by that much on the power available?"

Major Brant said shakily, "I think so."

"Then do it."

Commander Donahue said again, *"Toward* Jupiter?"

"Yes. Exactly. Io isn't the innermost of Jupiter's satellites. Amalthea is closer, Jupiter Five. If we can intersect its orbit properly, we can land on it. If we miss it, well, then, we will have hurried death by two hours."

Bigman felt a surge of sudden hope. He could never entirely despair while Lucky was in action, but until that moment he had not seen what it was that Lucky intended doing. He remembered now his earlier conversation with Lucky on the subject. The satellites were numbered in order of discovery. Amalthea was a small satellite, just a hundred miles in diameter, and it was discovered only after the four major satellites were known. So, though the closest to Jupiter, it was Jupiter Five. Somehow one tended to forget that. Because Io was called Jupiter One, there was always the tendency to think there was nothing between it and the planet itself.

And one hour later the *Jovian Moon* began a carefully plotted acceleration toward Jupiter, hastening toward the death trap.

They no longer centered the visiplate on any part of Jupiter. Though the latter swelled hourly, the center of sight remained on a portion of the star field a considerable distance from Jupiter's rim. The star field was under maximum magnification. At that point should be Jupiter Five, streaking for its rendezvous with a ship which was hurtling and straining down, down toward Jupiter. Either the ship would be caught by the speck of rock and saved, or it would miss and be lost forever.

"There it is," said Bigman in excitement. "That star shows a visible disk."

"Calculate observed position and motion," ordered Lucky, "and check with the computed orbit."

This was done.

"Any correction?" Lucky asked.

"We'll have to slow down by—"

"Never mind the figures. Do it!"

Jupiter Five circled Jupiter in twelve hours, moving in its orbit at a speed of nearly three thousand miles an hour. This was one and a half times as rapid as Io's motion and its gravitational field was only one twentieth that of Io. For both reasons, it made the harder target.

Major Brant's fists trembled on the controls as the all-important side thrusts bent the *Jovian Moon's* orbit ever so slightly to meet the onrushing Jupiter Five, slip behind it and round, matching speeds for just those vital moments that would enable the satellite's gravity to establish the ship in an orbit about itself.

Jupiter Five was a large, brilliant object now. If it stayed so, good. If it began to grow smaller, they had missed.

Major Brant whispered, "We've made it," and his head fell forward into his shaking palms as he released the controls.

Even Lucky closed his eyes momentarily in a kind of weary relief.

In one way the situation on Jupiter Five was far different from what it had been on Io. There, all the crew

had been sight-seers; the consideration of the heavens
had taken precedence over the leisurely preparations in
the valley.

Here on Jupiter Five, however, no one emerged
from the *Jovian Moon*. What there was to see, no one
saw.

The men stayed aboard the ship and worked on the
repair of the engines. Nothing else mattered. If they
failed, the landing on Jupiter Five could only postpone
doom and stretch it out into greater agony.

No normal ship could land on Jupiter Five to rescue
them, and no other Agrav ship existed or would exist
for a year at least. If they failed, there would be time
enough to watch Jupiter and the vision of the skies
while they waited for death.

Yet under less urgent conditions the vision would
have been worth watching. It was Io all over again
with everything doubled and tripled.

From the point at which the *Jovian Moon* landed,
Jupiter's lower rim seemed to sweep the flat, powdery
horizon. The giant looked so close in the airlessness
that a watcher would have imagined he could reach
out his hand and bury it in that circle of light.

From the horizon Jupiter stretched upward, halfway to zenith. At the moment the *Jovian Moon* landed,
Jupiter was almost full, and within the unbearable
circle of brilliant stripes and colors nearly ten thousand full moons Earth variety, could have been placed.
Almost one sixteenth of the entire vault of the sky
was covered by Jupiter.

And because Jupiter Five circled Jupiter in twelve
hours, the visible moons—there were four here rather
than three as on Io, since Io itself was now a moon—

moved three times as fast as they did on Io. So did all the stars and everything else in the sky, except for frozen Jupiter, which one side of the satellite eternally faced and which therefore never moved.

In five hours the sun would rise and it would be exactly the same in appearance as on Io; it would be the one thing that hadn't changed. But it would race toward a four-times-as-large Jupiter at three times the speed and make an eclipse a hundred times as terrifyingly beautiful.

But no one saw it. It took place twice while the *Jovian Moon* stayed and no one saw it. No one had the time. No one had the heart.

Panner finally sat down and stared out of bleary eyes. The flesh around them was red and puffy. His voice was a hoarse whisper.

"All right. Everyone to your normal stations. We'll have a dry run." He hadn't slept in forty hours. The others had worked in shifts, but Panner had stopped neither to eat nor to sleep.

Bigman, who had confined himself to unskilled labor, to fetching and carrying, to reading dials under direction and holding levers according to instruction, had no place in a dry run, no station, no duties. So he wandered somberly about the ship in search of Lucky and found him in the control room with Commander Donahue.

Lucky had his shirt off and was wiping his shoulders, forearms, and face on a large plastofluff towel.

As soon as he saw Bigman, he said briskly, "The ship will be moving, Bigman. We'll be taking off soon."

Bigman's eyes raised. "We're only doing a dry run, Lucky."

"It will work. That Jim Panner worked miracles."

Commander Donahue said stiffly, "Councilman Starr, you have saved my ship."

"No, no. Panner deserves the credit. I think half the engine is being held together with copper wire and mucilage, but it will work."

"You know what I mean, Councilman. You drove us on to Jupiter Five when the rest of us were ready to give up and panic. You saved my ship, and I will report that fact fully when I stand court-martial on Earth for having failed to co-operate with you on Jupiter Nine."

Lucky flushed in embarrassment. "I can't allow that, Commander. It is important that councilmen avoid publicity. As far as the official record is concerned, you will have remained in command at all times. There will be no mention of any actions of mine."

"Impossible. I couldn't allow myself to be praised for what you have done."

"You will have to. It's an order. And let's have no talk of court-martials."

Commander Donahue drew himself up with a kind of pride. "I deserve court-martial. You warned me of the presence of Sirian agents. I did not listen and as a result my ship was sabotaged."

"The blame is mine, too," Lucky said calmly. "I was on board ship and did not prevent it. Nevertheless, if we can bring back the saboteur, there will be no question of court-martial."

The commander said, "The saboteur, of course, is

the robot you warned me of. How I could be so blind!"

"I'm afraid you still don't see entirely. It wasn't the robot."

"*Not* the robot?"

"A robot could not have sabotaged the ship. It would have been bringing harm to humans and that would have meant breaking the First Law."

The commander frowned as he considered that. "It might not have been aware that it was doing harm."

"Everyone aboard ship, including the humanoid, understands Agrav. The robot would have known it was doing harm. In any case I think we have the identity of the saboteur, or will have in a moment."

"Oh? Who is he, Councilman Starr?"

"Well, consider this for a moment. If a man so sabotages a ship as to insure that it will either blow up or fall into Jupiter, he would be either a madman or a superhumanly dedicated person to stay on board that ship."

"Yes, I suppose so."

"Since the time we left Io, the air locks have never opened. If they had there would have been slight drops in air pressure, and the ship's barometer indicates no such drops. You see, then, the saboteur must never have gotten on the ship at Io. He's still there, unless he's been taken off."

"How could he be taken off? No ship could get to Io, except this one."

Lucky smiled grimly. "No *Earth* ship."

The commander's eyes widened. "Surely no Sirian ship, either."

"Are you sure?"

"Yes, I'm sure." The commander frowned. "And for that matter, wait a moment. Everyone reported on board before we left Io. We wouldn't have left without everyone reported present."

"In that case everyone is still on board."

"I would presume so."

"Well," said Lucky, "Panner has ordered all men to stations under emergency conditions. The whereabouts of every man should be fixed during this dry run. Call Panner and ask if anyone is missing."

Commander Donahue turned to the intercom, and signaled Panner.

There was some delay, and then Panner's voice, infinitely tired, answered. "I was about to call, Commander. The run was successful. We can take off. If we're lucky, things will hold till we're back on Jupiter Nine."

The commander said, "Very good. Your work will be properly acknowledged, Panner. Meanwhile, are all men at stations?"

Panner's face on the visiplate above the intercom seemed to harden all at once. *"No! By Space, I meant to tell you! We can't locate Summers."*

"Red Summers," Bigman cried in sudden excitement. "That murdering cobber. Lucky . . ."

"One moment, Bigman," Lucky said. "Dr. Panner, you mean Summers isn't in his quarters?"

"He isn't anywhere. Except that it's impossible, I'd say he wasn't on board."

"Thank you." Lucky reached over to break contact. "Well, Commander."

Bigman said, "Listen, Lucky. You remember once

I told you I met him coming out of the engine room? What was he doing down there?"

"We know now," said Lucky.

"And we know enough to get him," said the commander, white-faced. "We're landing on Io and . . ."

"Wait," said Lucky, "first things first. There is something more important even than a traitor."

"What?"

"The matter of the robot."

"That can wait."

"Perhaps not. Commander, you said that all men reported on board the *Jovian Moon* before we left Io. If so, the report was obviously a false one."

"Well?"

"I think we ought to try to find the source of the false report. A robot can't sabotage a ship, but if a man has sabotaged the ship without the robot's knowledge, it would be very simple for the robot to help that man remain off the ship if its help is requested."

"You mean whoever is responsible for the false report that Summers was on board ship is the robot?"

Lucky paused. He tried not to allow himself to grow too hopeful or feel too triumphant, and yet the argumen seemed perfect.

He said, "It seems so."

15

Traitor!

Commander Donahue said, "Major Levinson, then."
His eyes darkened. "And yet I find that impossible to
believe."

"Find what impossible to believe?" Lucky asked.

"That he is a robot. He's the man who took the report. He keeps our records. I know him well and I
swear that he *can't* be a robot."

"We'll question him, Commander. And one
thing—" Lucky's expression was somber. "Don't
accuse him of being a robot; don't ask him if he's one
or even imply that he might be one. Do nothing to
make him feel he's under suspicion."

The commander looked astonished. "Why not?"

"The Sirians have a way of protecting their robots.
Open suspicion may trigger some explosive device
within the major if he is indeed a robot."

The commander exhaled explosively. "Space!"

Major Levinson showed the signs of strain that were
universal among the men aboard the *Jovian Moon,*
but he stood at brisk military attention. "Yes, sir."

The commander said cautiously, "Councilman Starr has a few questions to ask."

Major Levinson shifted to face Lucky. He was quite tall, topping even Lucky's inches, with fair hair, blue eyes, and a narrow face.

Lucky said, "All men were reported on board the *Jovian Moon* at the time of take-off from Io, and you prepared that report. Is that right, major?"

"Yes, sir."

"Did you see each man individually?"

"No, sir. I used the intercom. Each man answered at take-off station or in his cabin."

"Each man? Did you hear each man's voice? Each individual voice?"

Major Levinson looked astonished. "I suppose so. That's not the sort of thing one remembers, really."

"Nevertheless it's quite important and I'm asking you to remember."

The major frowned and bent his head. "Well, now wait. Come to think of it, Norrich answered for Summers because Summers was in the bathroom." Then, with a sudden spark of excitement, he added, "Hold on, they're looking for Summers right now."

Lucky held up a palm. "Never mind that, Major. Would you get Norrich and send him up?"

Norrich came in on Major Levinson's arm. He looked bewildered. He said, "Commander, no one seems to be able to find Red Summers. What's happened to him?"

Lucky forestalled the commander's answer. He said, "We're trying to find out. Did you report Summers present when Major Levinson checked those aboard before we left Io?"

The blind engineer reddened. He said tightly, "Yes."

"The major says you said Summers was in the bathroom. Was he?"

"Well . . . No, he wasn't, Councilman. He had gotten off ship for a moment to pick up some item of equipment he had left behind. He didn't want the commander chewing him out—pardon me, sir—for carelessness, and he asked me to cover for him. He said he would be back well before take-off."

"Was he?"

"I . . . I thought . . . I had the impression he was. Mutt barked, I think, and I was sure Summers was coming back, but there isn't anything for me to do at take-off, so I was turning in for a nap and I guess I just didn't give the matter too much thought at the moment. Then there was the mess in the engine room almost right away, and after that there was no time to think of anything."

Panner's voice came over the central intercom with sudden loudness. "Warning to all men. We are taking off. Everyone to stations."

The *Jovian Moon* was in space again, lifting itself against Jupiter's gravity with powerful surges. It was expending energy at a rate that would have bankrupted five ordinary vessels and only the faint tremor in the sound of the hyperatomics remained to show that the ship's mechanism depended, in part, on makeshift devices.

Panner gloomily pondered on the poor showing the ship would now make energy-wise. He said, "As is, I'll get back with only seventy per cent of original energy, when it could have been eighty-five or ninety.

If we land on Io and make another take-off, we'll get back with only fifty. And I don't know if we can stand another take-off."

But Lucky said, "We must get Summers, and you know why."

With Io growing large-sized once again in the visiplate, Lucky said thoughtfully, "It's not entirely certain we can find him, Bigman."

Bigman said incredulously, "You don't think the Sirians actually picked him up, do you?"

"No, but Io's a big place. If he wanders off to some rendezvous, we might never locate him. I'm counting on his staying put. He'd have to carry air, food, and water with him if he moved, so it would be most logical for him to stay put. Particularly when he'd have no reason to expect us to come back."

Bigman said, "We should have known it was that cobber all along, Lucky. He tried to kill you first thing. Why should he want to do that, if he weren't playing along with the Sirians?"

"True enough, Bigman, but remember this: we were looking for a spy. Summers couldn't be the spy. He had no access to the leaked information. Once it was clear to me that the spy was a robot, that cleared Summers on another account. The V-frog had detected emotion in him, so he couldn't be a robot and therefore couldn't be the spy. Of course that didn't prevent him from being a traitor and saboteur, and I should not have allowed the search for a spy to blind me to that possibility."

He shook his head and added, "This seems to be a case riddled with disappointment. If it had been anyone else *but* Norrich who had covered for Summers, we would have had our robot. The trouble is that Norrich is the only man who could have had convincingly innocent reason to co-operate with Summers. He was friendly with Summers; we know that. Then, too, Norrich could innocently be ignorant that Summers never returned before take-off. After all, he's blind."

Bigman said, "Besides which, he showed emotion, too, so he can't be the robot."

Lucky nodded. "True enough." Yet he frowned and grew silent.

Down, down they came to Io's surface, landing almost in the marks of their previous take-off. The dots and smeared shadows in the valley resolved themselves into the equipment they had set up as they approached.

Lucky was surveying the surface intently through the visiplate. "Were any air tights left behind on Io?"

"No," said the commander.

"Then we may have our man. One air tight, as you may notice, is fully expanded behind that rock formation. Do you have the list of material unaccounted for on board?"

The commander delivered a sheet of paper without comment, and Lucky studied it. He said, "Bigman and I will go out after him. I doubt that we'll need help."

The tiny sun was high in the sky, and Bigman and Lucky walked on their own shadows. Jupiter was a thinnish crescent.

Lucky spoke on Bigman's wave length. "He must have seen the ship unless he's sleeping."

"Or unless he's gone," said Bigman.

"I doubt that he's gone."

And almost at once Bigman cried, "Sands of Mars, Lucky, look up there!"

A figure appeared at the top of the line of rock. It stood out blackly against the thinning yellow line of Jupiter.

"Don't move," came a low, tired voice on Lucky's own wave length. "I'm holding a blaster."

"Summers," said Lucky, "come down and surrender."

A note of bitter mockery entered the other's strained voice. "I guessed the right wave length, didn't I, Councilman? Though it was an easy guess from the size of your friend . . . Get back to your ship or I'll kill you both."

Lucky said, "Don't bluff pointlessly. At this distance you couldn't hit us in a dozen tries."

Bigman added with tenor fury, "And I'm armed, too, and I can hit you even at *this* distance. Just remember that and don't even move a finger near the activating button."

Lucky said, "Throw down your blaster and surrender."

"Never!" said Summers.

"Why not? To whom are you being loyal?" Lucky demanded. "The Sirians? Did they promise to pick you up? If so, they lied to you and betrayed you. They're not worth loyalty. Tell me where the Sirians' base in the Jupiter system is located."

"You know so much! Figure it out for yourself."

"What subwave combination do you use to contact them?"

"Figure that out, too . . . Don't move any closer."

Lucky said, "Help us out now, Summers, and I'll do my best to get you mild treatment on Earth."

Summers laughed weakly. "The word of a councilman?"

"Yes."

"I wouldn't take it. Get back to your ship."

"Why have you turned against your own world, Summers? What have the Sirians offered you? Money?"

"Money!" The other's voice was suddenly furious. "Do you want to know what they offered me? I'll tell you. A chance at a decent life." They could hear the tiny gritting sound Summers made as his teeth ground together. "What did I have on Earth? Misery all my life. A crowded planet with no decent chance at making a name and a position for myself. Everywhere I went I was surrounded by millions of people clawing at each other for existence, and when I tried to claw also, I was put in jail. I made up my mind that if ever I could do anything to get back at Earth, I would."

"What do you expect to get from Sirius in the way of a decent life?"

"They invited me to emigrate to the Sirian planets, if you must know." He paused, and his breathing made small whistling noises. "New worlds out there. Clean worlds. There's room for men there; they need men and talent. I'd have a chance there."

"You'll never get there. When are they coming for you?"

Summers was silent.

Lucky said, "Face it, man. They're not coming for you. They have no decent life for you; no life at all for you. Only death for you. You expected them before this, didn't you?"

"I didn't."

"Don't lie. It won't improve the situation for you. We've checked the supplies missing from the *Jovian Moon*. We know exactly how much oxygen you smuggled off the ship. Oxygen cylinders are clumsy things to carry even under Io's gravity when you have to sneak them off without being caught and in a hurry. Your air supply is almost gone now, isn't it?"

"I have plenty of air," said Summers.

Lucky said, "I say it's almost gone. Don't you see the Sirians aren't coming for you? They can't come for you without Agrav and they haven't got Agrav. Great Galaxy, man, have you let yourself get so hungry for the Sirian worlds that you'll let them kill you in as open and crude a double-cross as I've ever seen? Now, tell me, what have you done for them?"

Summers said, "I did what they asked me to do and that wasn't much. And if I have any regrets," he shouted in sudden, breathless bravado, "it's only that I didn't get the *Jovian Moon*. How did you get away, anyway? I fixed it. I *fixed* the rotten, slimy . . ." he ended, choking.

Lucky motioned to Bigman and broke into the soaring lope characteristic of running on low-gravity worlds. Bigman followed, veering off so as not to offer a single target.

Summers' blaster came up and made a thin popping sound, all that was possible in Io's thin wisps of atmosphere. Sand kicked up and around, and a crater formed yards from Lucky's fleeting figure.

"You won't catch me," Summers yelled with a kind

of weak violence. "I'm not coming back to Earth. They'll come for me. The Sirians will come for me."

"Up, Bigman," said Lucky. He had reached the rock formation. Jumping upward, he caught a projection and hurled himself further upward. At sixth-normal gravity, a man, even in a space suit, could outdo a mountain goat in climbing.

Summers screamed thinly. His hands moved up to his helmet and he leaped backward and disappeared.

Lucky and Bigman reached the top. The rock formation was nearly sheer on the other side, with sharp outcroppings breaking the clifflike face. Summers was a spread-eagled figure, dropping slowly downward, striking against the face of the rock, and rebounding.

Bigman said, "Let's get him, Lucky," and jumped far outward, wide of the cliff. Lucky followed.

It would have been a killing leap on Earth, even on Mars. On Io it was little more than a tooth-jarring drop.

They hit with bent knees and let themselves roll to take up some of the force of impact. Lucky was on his feet first and made for Summers, who lay prone and unmoving.

Bigman came up panting. "Hey, that wasn't the easiest jump I— What's the matter with the cobber?"

Lucky said grimly. "He's dead. I knew his oxygen was low from the way he sounded. He was almost unconscious. It's why I rushed him."

"You could go a long time being unconscious," said Bigman.

Lucky shook his head. "He made sure. He really didn't want to be taken. Just before he jumped, he opened his helmet to Io's poison air and he hit the cliff."

He stepped aside and Bigman caught a glimpse of the smashed face.

Lucky said, "Poor fool!"

"Poor *traitor!*" Bigman raged. "He might have had the answer and he wouldn't tell us. Now he can't tell us."

Lucky said, "He doesn't have to, Bigman. I think I know the answer now."

16

Robot!

"You do?" The little Martian's voice rose to a squeak. "What is it, Lucky?"

But Lucky said, "Not now." He gazed down at Summers, whose dead eyes stared sightlessly toward the alien heavens. He said, "Summers has one distinction. He is the first man ever to die on Io."

He looked up. The sun was edging behind Jupiter. The planet was becoming only a faint silvery circle of twilit atmosphere.

Lucky said, "It will be dark. Let's go back to the ship."

Bigman paced the floor of their cabin. It took only three steps one way, three steps the other, but he paced. He said, "But if you *know*, Lucky, why don't you . . ."

Lucky said, "I can't take ordinary action and risk explosion. Let me do it in my own time and my own way, Bigman."

There was a firmness in his tone that quite subdued Bigman. He changed the subject and said, "Well, then, why waste any more time on Io because of that cobber out there? He's dead. There's nothing more to do about him."

"One thing," said Lucky. The door signal flashed and he added, "Open it, Bigman. It should be Norrich."

It was. The blind engineer stepped in, his dog, Mutt, going before.

Norrich's blue, unseeing eyes blinked rapidly. He said, "I've heard about Summers, Councilman. It's a terrible thing to think he tried to . . . to . . . Terrible that he was a traitor. Yet somehow I'm sorry for him."

Lucky nodded. "I knew you would be. It's why I asked you to come here. It's dark out on Io now. The sun's in eclipse. When the eclipse is over, will you come out with me to bury Summers?"

"Gladly. We should do that much for any man, shouldn't we?" Norrich's hand dropped as if for consolation on Mutt's muzzle, and the dog came close and moved softly against his master as though feeling some dim need to offer sympathy.

Lucky said, "I thought you would want to come along. After all, you were his friend. You might want to pay your last respects."

"Thank you. I would like to." Norrich's blind eyes were moist.

Lucky said to Commander Donahue just before he placed the helmet over his head, "It will be our last trip out. When we return, we will take off for Jupiter Nine."

"Good," the commander said, and there seemed some unspoken understanding as their eyes met.

Lucky put on his helmet and in another corner of the pilot room, Norrich's sensitive fingers moved delicately over Mutt's flexible space suit, making sure all fastenings were secure. Inside the glass-fronted, odd-shaped helmet that fitted over Mutt's head, Mutt's jaws moved in a faintly heard bark. It was obvious the dog knew he was headed for a trip into low gravity and that he enjoyed the prospect.

The first grave on Io was done. It had been dug out of hard, rocky soil by the use of force diggers. It was filled in with a mound of gravel and topped by an oval boulder as a marker.

The three men stood round it while Mutt wandered off in the distance, trying vainly, as always, to examine his surroundings, though metal and glass blocked the use of his sense of smell.

Bigman, who knew what Lucky expected him to do but didn't know why, waited tensely.

Norrich stood with his head bowed and said softly, "This was a man who wanted something very much, did wrong for that reason, and has paid for it."

"He did what the Sirians asked him to do," Lucky added. "That was his crime. He committed sabotage and . . ."

Norrich stiffened as the pause in Lucky's remarks lengthened. He said, "And *what?*"

"And he got *you* on board ship. He refused to join the crew without you. You yourself told me that it was only through him that you were assigned to the *Jovian Moon.*"

Lucky's voice grew stern. "You are a robot spy placed here by the Sirians. Your blindness makes you seem innocent to the others on the project, but you don't need a sense of sight. You killed the V-frog and covered for Summers to get him off the ship. Your own death meant nothing to you in the face of orders, as Third Law states. And, finally, you fooled me by the display of emotion I caught through the V-frog, a synthetic emotion built into you by the Sirians."

This was the cue for which Bigman had been waiting. Lifting the butt of his blaster high, he hurled himself at Norrich, whose incoherent protestations did not coalesce into words.

"I knew it was you," Bigman shrieked, "and I'm smashing you."

"It's not true," Norrich wailed, finding his voice. He threw up his hands and stumbled backward.

And suddenly Mutt was a streak in the pale, white light. He hurled himself furiously across the quarter mile that separated him from the men, aiming with desperate passion at Bigman.

Bigman paid no attention. One hand caught at Norrich's shoulder. The other swung the blaster upward.

Then Mutt collapsed!

While he was still ten feet from the struggling pair, his legs stiffened uselessly and he tumbled and rolled past them, coming to a frozen halt at last. Through the glass of his helmet his jaws could be seen hanging open, as though in mid-bark.

Bigman held his threatening position over Norrich as though he, too, were frozen.

Lucky approached the animal with quick steps. He used his force shovel as a kind of unwieldy knife and slit Mutt's space suit lengthwise from neck to tail.

Then, tensely, he slit through the skin at the back of the neck and probed deftly with his mail-shod fingers. They closed on a small sphere that was not bone. He lifted the sphere and met resistance. Holding his breath, he snapped the wires that held it in place and stood up, almost weak with relief. The base of the brain had been the logical place for a mechanism to be activated by the brain, and he had found it. Mutt could endanger no one now.

Norrich cried out, as though through instinctive knowledge of his loss.

"My dog! What are you doing to my dog?"

Lucky said softly, "It's no dog, Norrich. Never was. It was a robot. Come, Bigman, lead him back to the ship. I'll carry Mutt."

Lucky and Bigman were in Panner's room. The *Jovian Moon* was in flight again, and Io was falling rapidly away, already only a bright coin in the sky.

"What gave it away?" said Panner.

Lucky said somberly, "A number of things which I never saw. Every clue pointed firmly to Mutt, but I was so intent on finding a humanoid robot, so inwardly convinced that a robot had to look human, that I looked past the truth though it stared me in the face."

"Then when *did* you see?"

"When Summers killed himself by jumping off the rock. I stared at him, lying there, and thought of Bigman falling through the ammonia snow and nearly dying. I thought: There's no Mutt that can save this one. . . . And that did it."

"How? I don't understand."

"How *did* Mutt save Bigman? When the dog came running up past us, Bigman was somewhere under the ice, nowhere to be seen. Yet Mutt plunged in, made for Bigman without hesitation, and dragged him out. We accepted that without thought because we somehow expect dogs to find what can't be seen through their sense of smell. But Mutt's head was enclosed. He could neither see nor smell Bigman, yet had no trouble locating him. We ought to have seen that unusual sense perception was involved. We'll find out exactly which when our roboticists work over the carcass."

"Now that you explain," said Panner, "it looks plain enough. The dog had to give itself away because First Law compelled it not to allow a human being to come to harm."

"That's right," said Lucky. "Once suspicions of Mutt finally penetrated, a few other things started falling into place. Summers had maneuvered Norrich on board, yes, but in doing so, he also got Mutt on board. Moreover, Summers was the one who got Mutt for Norrich in the first place. The chances are that there is a spy ring on Earth whose only task is to distribute these robot dogs to people working in or near critical research centers.

"Dogs are perfect spies. If you find a dog nosing through your papers or walking through a super-secret section of a laboratory, are you concerned? Chances are you pet the dog and feed him a dog biscuit. I checked through Mutt as best I could and I think he has a built-in subetheric transmitter which keeps him in contact with his Sirian masters. They can see what he sees, hear what he hears. For instance, they saw the V-frog through Mutt's eyes, recognized its danger, and directed him to kill it. He could be made to handle an energy projector with which to fuse the lock of a door. Even if he was caught in the act, there was a good chance we would put it all down to the accidental happenings of a dog playing with a weapon he had found.

"But once all this had occurred to me, I was only at the beginning of the practical problem. I had to try to take the dog intact. I was sure that any obvious suspicion of Mutt would trigger an explosion inside him. So first I brought Norrich and Mutt to a safe distance from the ship by suggesting we dig Summers' grave. In that way if Mutt did explode, the ship, at least, and its men would escape. Naturally I left a note with Commander Donahue, to be opened in case I did not return, so that Earth would at least investigate dogs in research centers.

"I then accused Norrich . . ."

Bigman broke in, "Sands of Mars, Lucky, for a while I thought you really meant it when you said Norrich had killed the V-frog and fooled us with built-in emotion."

Lucky shook his head. "No, Bigman. If he could fool us with built-in emotion, why bother to kill the V-frog? No, I was making sure that if Sirians were listening through Mutt's senses, they would be convinced I was on the wrong track. In addition, I was setting up a situation for Mutt's benefit.

"You see, Bigman, under instructions, attacked Norrich. As a Seeing Eye dog, Mutt was built with strong orders to defend his master against attack, and obedience to orders are Second Law. Usually there's no problem here. Few people attack a blind man and those who do will usually stop if the dog simply growls and bares its fangs.

"But Bigman persisted in his attack, and Mutt, for the first time since being built, had to carry through all the way. But how could he? He couldn't hurt Bigman. First Law. Yet he couldn't allow Norrich to be hurt either. It was a complete dilemma and Mutt went out of commission. Once that happened, I gambled that any bomb he contained could no longer be triggered. So I removed it and after that we were safe."

Panner took a deep breath. "Very neat."

Lucky snorted. "Neat? I could have done this the first day I landed on Jupiter Nine, if I had my wits about me. I almost had it, at that. The thought was at the edge of my mind constantly and I never caught it."

Bigman said, "What was it, Lucky? I still don't know."

"It was simple enough. The V-frog detected animal emotion as well as human emotion. We had an example of that when we first landed on Jupiter Nine. We detected hunger in the mind of a cat. Then, later, we met Norrich and he urged you to aim a blow at him in order to show off Mutt's protectiveness. You did so. I detected Norrich's emotions and yours, Bigman, through the V-frog, but although Mutt showed every outward sign of anger, I detected no trace of such an emotion. There was the absolute proof as early as that, that Mutt had no emotions and was therefore no dog but a robot. Yet I was so convinced that I was looking for some human that my mind refused to see that point. . . . Well, let's go to dinner and visit Norrich on the way. I want to promise him that we'll get him another dog, a real one."

They arose, and Bigman said, "Anyway, Lucky, maybe it took some time, but we've stopped the Sirians."

Lucky said quietly, "I don't know that we've stopped them, but certainly we've slowed them down."

OUTER SPACE